Staghorn

Staghorn

TIM CHAMPLIN

Sagebrush
Large Print Westerns

Library of Congress Cataloging-in-Publication Data

Champlin, Tim, 1937—
    Staghorn / Tim Champlin.
        p.   cm.
    ISBN 1-57490-328-4 (lg. print: hardcover)
    1. River boats—Fiction. 2. Gamblers—Fiction. 3. Large
    type books. I. Title

PS3553.H265 S73 2001
813'.54—dc21   00-051001

Cataloguing in Publication Data is available from
the British Library and the National Library of Australia.

Sagebrush Large Print Westerns are published in the United
States and Canada by Thomas T. Beeler, Publisher, PO Box 659,
Hampton Falls, New Hampshire 03844-0659. ISBN 1-57490-328-4

Published in the United Kingdom, Eire, and the Republic of
South Africa by Isis Publishing Ltd, 7 Centremead, Osney
Mead, Oxford OX2 0ES England. ISBN 0-7531-6437-X

Published in Australia and New Zealand by Bolinda Publishing
Pty Ltd, 17 Mohr Street, Tullamarine, Victoria, Australia, 3043
ISBN 1-74030-294-X

Manufactured by Sheridan Books in Chelsea, Michigan.

CHAPTER 1

THEY WERE STILL THERE, THE TWO THINGS I remembered best and liked least about Wyoming—the powdery dust and the incessant wind. As we stepped down stiffly from the stagecoach in Cheyenne, that dust and that wind welcomed us in the form of a swirling, yellow-gray fog. Gritty, eye-stinging, and suffocating, it was a rude shock after the cool freshness of the forested Black Hills. It was only late May, but the high plains already showed signs of a long, dry summer ahead. Even ankle-deep mud would have been preferable to this.

This same dry wind had caused the town of Deadwood to burn to the ground only a couple of weeks before. If Hell is really an unquenchable fire, I'm going to do my darnedest to be sure I don't go there, after experiencing the roaring inferno that leveled that wooden boomtown. My eyebrows were just beginning to grow back, my singed hair was much shorter than usual, and the high-pitched ringing in my ears had only recently subsided—all the results of being too close to a dynamite explosion during that fire. I also suspected that I had cracked a rib or two, because the normal soreness from that blast would have gone away by now, but I still felt some pain in the rib cage area when I moved certain ways.

Wiley Jenkins was handing my leather valise out of the rear boot of the stage as I tried to shield my face and keep my mouth closed against the choking dust that swirled up from the street around the coach. Wiley got his own grip and bedroll, and we trudged off without a

1

word toward the nearest hotel. It was coming on to suppertime, and we were both exhausted by our three-day trip from the Black Hills. Even though Wells Fargo had lost its depot in the recent fire, they had managed to save the two coaches that were in town, and all their horses. Working out of a makeshift tent office, they had resumed service only two days after the fire. But we had delayed our own departure for two weeks to attend the wedding of Wiley's sister, Cathy, to Curtis Wilder, former captain in the third Cavalry. The four of us had been partners. Then Cathy and Curtis fell in love and married. Now it was time for Wiley and me to move on. We had asked the newlyweds to manage our small placer claim and to take out whatever gold remained in it.

Wiley and I took our share of the reward money that Wells Fargo had paid us for helping capture a gang of stage robbers and decided to try our luck in the Arizona Territory. I had resigned my job as a war correspondent for the *Chicago Times Herald* a few months earlier, but with my share of the placer dust, along with some of the reward money and Wiley's modest inheritance from his father, we hoped to have enough to see us through until something else turned up. Both of us were single and footloose. Wiley was in his late twenties, a former mule-packer with General Buck's expedition and an athletic young man who had done nearly every type of unskilled job the West had to offer, from mucking in the mines to grading roadbed for the Union Pacific. Two years of college in his native Kentucky just after the war had given him a literate background, and he was constantly devouring every bit of reading material he could find on the book-poor frontier. When I first met him a year ago, he impressed me as a cynical know-it-all who drank too much, but it didn't take long for me to learn what he really was. Far from being cynical, he had never lost his sense of wonder at objects and people around him.

We were both too tired to talk as we shouldered our way through the sidewalk traffic to the brick hotel. Cheyenne had grown bigger and noisier in the few months since I had last seen it. The railroad was the main reason for its growth, in addition to Fort D. A. Russell, just outside of town. But, in spite of the look of permanence its buildings were beginning to acquire, the place still had the feel of a raw, brawling frontier town, swarming with transients. Cheyenne was still an unlovely place with no nearby hills, lakes, or woods to soften its appearance. Built hurriedly in this unfortunate location, the town was exposed to all the harsh extremes of high plains weather. Wagons and horses churned the dust in summer and plowed up the mud, slush, and snow of its streets in winter.

We registered at the hotel, dropped our gear, and headed for a public bathhouse to soak away some of our accumulated grime and fatigue and get a shave. Two hours later we were finally seated in a restaurant with a late supper of venison steaks and fried potatoes in front of us.

"You know," Wiley was saying, "Victorio and Geronimo have been on a rampage in the southern part of Arizona. Maybe we ought to come into the territory from the north and drop down toward the Silver King Mine. Stick to the cover of the mountains as much as possible. There are a few small white settlements and ranches and army posts scattered through the area." He grinned around a mouthful of food. "Listen to me— talking like it's a day's ride between these places. What I've seen of it, it's mostly just a vast wilderness—miles

3

and miles of mountain and desert. Beautiful but dangerous. It's been about three years since I was down that way, but I doubt if it's changed a whole lot. We could take the train farther west, and then buy a couple of horses, or maybe start out from here with a wagon, and buy a couple of good mounts later on . . ." He paused and gave me a searching look. "Are you all right?" he asked, suddenly interrupting himself as he noticed my vacant look.

"Just a little run-down. I'll be all right."

"Ribs still bothering you?"

"Some."

"You ought to have a doctor check that ear, too. It looks infected."

"I think I will. It's been oozing a lot. Hasn't been healing right. May need to be cleaned out again and stitched."

I shuddered as I remembered the bullet that had taken off my left earlobe. It might easily have taken my head. I could still see the black bore of the .45, the look of murderous hate, the light of the flaming buildings reflecting from the gunman's glasses in that eternal instant as I stood frozen in my tracks, waiting to die. If his horse hadn't shied just as he pulled the trigger, the name of Matt Tierney would now be decorating a tombstone in Mount Moriah Cemetery.

I came out of my reverie and realized that Wiley was still looking at me curiously. "Oh, I'm sorry. What were you saying?"

"Nothing."

He continued to stare at me as I helped myself to another wedge of corn bread. I began to feel uncomfortable under his scrutiny. "What's wrong?" I asked.

"You know, maybe we should postpone this trip to Arizona," he replied. And then, after a pause, "You don't really seem like you're up to it just yet."

"I'm all right," I exaggerated, trying to smile. In fact, I felt physically and emotionally drained, in spite of the hot bath and the food that was just beginning to pick me up.

"No." Wiley shook his head. "We don't need to be going into Apache country unless we're both in top shape. I think we need a little vacation first. We've got the money. How about a trip back East? Maybe Chicago? You could look up some of your old friends. It's been over a year since you were home."

I didn't want to hold Wiley back from heading west, but the idea of a rest was most welcome to me. I didn't object. "I don't have any relatives in Chicago. And my friends won't miss me. Chicago can wait. How about New Orleans? I've always wanted to see that city."

Wiley grinned that boyish grin. "You know, I've traveled a good bit of the South, but I've never made it there either. I hear a man's education is never complete until he's seen New Orleans."

The way Wiley warmed to the subject, I really believe he was as ready for a little relaxation as I was.

"As soon as we finish up here, why don't we take a little stroll over to the depot and take a look at their eastbound schedule."

His suggestion was spoken with a finality that left no room for argument.

CHAPTER 2

"MAN, AM I STUFFED!" WILEY JENKINS SIGHED, shoving back from the table and dropping his napkin onto the chinaware. "If we keep eating like we have been for the last three weeks, I'll weigh two hundred before we get to Saint Louis. I can hardly get my pants buttoned now."

"Let's take a stroll up on the hurricane deck," I suggested. "I need to shake down some of this food and get some fresh air. It's hot in here."

We were nearly twelve hours out of New Orleans on the *Silver Swan,* a huge, side-wheel packet, built only two years before, in 1875. It was a boat that rivaled the *Grand Republic* for size and luxury. The mess boys moved in to clear the tables as the diners began to disperse toward the bar, their staterooms, or the promenade deck. We sauntered toward the forward end of the long saloon to reach the stairs to the hurricane deck. Wiley cast a longing glance at the bar as we passed.

"I'm even too full for an after-dinner brandy," he groaned, slipping his belt open a notch. "I don't think I've ever eaten soup, beefsteak, baked pork, platters of duck, cold meats, potatoes, rice, yams, beans, corn bread, rice pudding, tarts, and rum—not to mention about five different kinds of French sauces—all at one meal before. The roustabouts will have a good grub pile of leftovers tonight." He paused and looked back at the long saloon. "Whew! Look at that! I'll bet there's not a hotel in America as elegant as this boat."

I had to agree. I had been in some beautiful hotels in

6

both New York and Chicago, but none of them compared to the *Silver Swan* and its showpiece—a 280-foot-long saloon. It was a marvel of gingerbread and latticework and gilt. Crystal chandeliers held oil lamps whose chimneys were covered by hand-painted globes. The white paneling and mirrors made the room appear even larger, and the light of the westering sun, lancing through the skylights, sparkled on the crystal goblets, mirrors, and chandeliers. Rows of white colonnades on either side of the long cabin separated it from the spacious storerooms on each side. The furniture was all heavy dark wood and red leather. An ornate carpet covered the entire floor, muffling the sound of the many feet. The strains of a Viennese waltz could be heard from the pianist at the grand piano in the aft end of the cabin.

"Beats the hell out of Deadwood, anyway," Wiley remarked as we climbed the stairs, "and it's as good as anything we saw in New Orleans."

"A real floating palace," I concurred.

Wiley and I had thoroughly enjoyed our two weeks of relaxing and sight-seeing in New Orleans before starting upriver toward the new silver strikes in the Arizona Territory.

We reached the open air of the next level and strolled aft along the starboard side, where the upper level cabins were set aside for the captain and crew.

"Your ear's almost all healed up," Wiley observed, glancing at me. "Although you're going to be a little short on that side."

I reached up to the flaking scab where my left earlobe used to be. " 'Fraid so." A chill went over me at the recollection of that wild night only a month ago in the Black Hills. I stared down at the dark green water being

7

churned up in our wake. "I never dreamed, a year ago, that all these things would happen to me. But it still beats being bored to death as a newspaper reporter in Chicago." I paused and stared out over the water again. "Sometimes I wonder if a man really has control of his destiny. If my parents hadn't fled Ireland when I was only ten years old, who knows where I'd be now? Maybe dead. I was already trying to join a gang of young street-fighters who thought they were going to whip the British all by themselves."

"Seems like there's fighting just about everywhere. I wonder how the campaign against the Sioux and Northern Cheyenne is going since we skedaddled from General Buck's outfit last year? I haven't been following the newspapers."

"Devastating. The Indians are just fighting a rear-guard action. It's only a matter of time."

"You know, all of that seems so far away right now," Wiley said with a contented sigh as he shrugged out of his black coat and loosened his tie. I had already accommodated myself to the humid heat by shedding the jacket I had worn to dinner and rolling up the sleeves of my white shirt.

We ambled past the housing of the starboard paddle wheel, looking aft out over the sweep of river bending out of sight a half mile behind us. Even though I could see little of the river from where I stood, I knew that the solid wall of trees along each shoreline and the wilderness of tangled brush and trees hung with Spanish moss farther back screened the marshy swamp of this Louisiana lowland. The whole area looked as if no human being had ever set foot in it.

We turned and started up the port side of the hurricane deck, feeling the slight breeze created by the

8

forward motion of the boat. It felt good against my damp skin.

The explosive puffing of steam escaping through the tall pipes grew less noisy as we walked forward.

> *"Then away, my love, away,*
> *Awaaay for Rio!*
> *The biscuits is weevily,*
> *And the salthorse is tough,*
> *And we're bound to the Rio Grande . . ."*

The low sound of the song reached our ears over the noise of escaping steam and the churning of the paddle wheels. The only other person on this side of the deck was a few yards ahead of us. He was a young man who stood with one foot propped on the low rail, facing west and leaning forward with both elbows on his knee.

> *". . . ever down to the Rio Grande?*
> *That river flows down golden sands.*
> *Awaaay for Rio!"*

The voice was low, as if he sang to himself, but the haunting refrain carried clearly to us. Then he raised a harmonica to his mouth and the sounds of the song sprang expertly from the mouth harp.

"The Rio Grande's a long way from here," Wiley said to him as we approached.

He stopped playing and looked around, blankly, as if we had interrupted some deep thought.

"What's that?" he finally said.

"You were singing of the Rio Grande. We're probably over 500 miles from it right now."

"A lot farther than that," he answered. "That chantey

9

refers to the Rio Grande do Sul in Brazil." He straightened up and faced us, slipping the instrument into his shirt pocket. He was about five nine and fairly muscular, though slim. I guessed his normal weight to be about 160, but he looked lighter than that now. A worn, haggard look about the eyes made his young face seem older. His hair was thick and shaggy blond, and from what I could see, in the light of the setting sun, his eyes were a greenish brown. He was dressed in dark cotton pants and a white shirt with no collar or tie, an attire that reflected the weather, rather than any social norm.

He stood there looking us over, not saying anything else.

Wiley seemed somewhat taken aback.

"Nice view," he said lamely, nodding toward the reddening sunset.

"Yeah." The young man turned away and propped his foot on the rail once more.

"Going far upriver?"

"Eastern Dakota," came the short reply.

"Business or pleasure?" Wiley inquired.

"Going home."

Clearly the man was not inclined to talk. He continued to stare toward the shore where the darkening line of trees slid past. The sun had dulled to an orange disk that rested atop the horizon, casting a sheen of red, shading upward to rose, in the expanse of sky. The color was duplicated in the flat sheet of flowing river below us.

I was willing to let our attempt at friendliness drop, but Wiley persisted. He was constantly doing things like this on some whim or other—nosing into the affairs of other people, even total strangers, especially if the

10

person appeared unusual in some way. It was a practice that could get a man shot. I often thought Wiley had more of an instinct for news than I did. Or maybe I was just more circumspect. Wiley was not a pushy individual by nature—just interested in, and often critical of, his fellow man. He had a childlike quality of wonder at everything around him. The blasé, hard-drinking, worldly-wise attitude he had affected when I first met him over a year ago had proven to be just that—an affectation. It was not the real Wiley Jenkins.

He had propped a boot up on the rail, also, and was looking off to the west, still talking.

"You say that song was a chantey? Are you a sailor?"

The stranger did not reply and obviously preferred to be let alone. He pulled out his mouth harp and began to play again. I was uncomfortable and kept sidling away, trying to catch. Wiley's eye.

I failed to dislodge him, and after a minute or two, as he kept up his one-sided conversation, I gave up and walked away, retreating to the bar below for a taste of brandy. The bar was crowded, since the boat was loaded to capacity, carrying over 120 cabin passengers. An untold number of deck passengers, mostly poor Irish and Norwegian immigrants, were jammed down, below among the cotton bales, whiskey barrels, cordwood, and whatever other cargo was aboard. But, of course, they weren't allowed on the cabin deck.

I leaned on the bar, sipping the amber liquid in the tiny glass, savoring the pungent fumes that helped clear my sinuses.

The dishes had been cleared away quickly and the tablecloths removed. The lamps in the chandeliers were being lighted as dusk began to dim the long saloon. Two or three tables of men playing poker had already

11

formed, ignoring the prominent sign that forbade any gambling by order of the owners. Aside from sight-seeing, reading, and possibly lovemaking, what else was there to do on a passage of several days, except gamble, and eat and sleep? As long as there were no disturbances, even professional gamblers were allowed to operate, Wiley had told me.

I turned back toward the bar, and there stood Wiley at my elbow, signaling the bartender for a brandy.

"No luck with the stranger?"

"None. Like talking to a rock. Too bad. He looks like an interesting character."

There was a general stir in the cabin, and Wiley and I turned around to see what was happening.

"Who's that?" Wiley wanted to know.

"The crown prince of Rumania," I replied, watching the group of five men moving among the tables in the saloon.

"The *what*?" Wiley asked sarcastically.

"I'm not joking. That fellow with the embroidered vest and the yellow silk shirt is Prince Ferdinand Zarahoff, eldest son of the monarch of Rumania, and heir to the throne."

He looked at me sideways. "You're crazy."

"No. You were already asleep in your cabin early this morning when he and his party came aboard, just before we left New Orleans. See what you miss when you stay up all night, carousing?"

Wiley gave me a sour look and sipped his brandy. "It was our last night in New Orleans and I couldn't waste it. How come I didn't see him at supper?"

"I imagine he and his party dined with the captain up in the Texas."

"Huh. What's he doing in this country?"

12

"Well, you know European royalty. They're constantly coming over here to get a taste of the American West. I read in the paper yesterday that he's even got Buffalo Bill Cody lined up to give him a tour and take his party on a buffalo hunt."

"The idle rich—always looking to be entertained."

"Wouldn't you trade places with him?"

"Well . . . maybe. If I didn't have to face being a king someday. Somebody's always gunning for them."

"As I recall, you're not presently employed," I reminded him. "You've got a pretty good stake from our placer mine in the Black Hills, a share of the Wells Fargo reward, and part of your father's inheritance. Seems to me you've got the best of both—leisure *and* money."

"You're talking about real wealth when you discuss royalty—not just a temporary stake. I'll probably have to go to work at something before too long."

"Well, at least he's not puttin' on the dog like most of these dukes and princes and earls. His whole retinue consists of the four men you see with him. Hell, Custer used to travel with more servants than that."

"Custer thought he *was* royalty."

As we talked, the saloon began to fill again with passengers. Some of them were being driven inside by the mosquitoes, but the majority came to smoke, drink, socialize, and gamble. We stayed at the bar to take advantage of the slight breeze coming through the open door a few feet away.

We discussed our plans for continuing on toward the Arizona Territory, still pleased with the sudden decision, made a month ago, to reward ourselves with some luxury and civilized living before tackling another raw frontier area. We were both in much better shape now and raring to go.

13

"Shall we stop in Saint Louis and go overland from there, or get a river packet as far as Saint Joe?"

"I'm in favor of going as far as we can by river. Saint Louis is pure hell in the summertime, and I'm sure to spend more money if we stop there."

"Okay by me. This kind of travel sure beats a train or stage."

"Those Missouri River stern-wheelers are not nearly as fancy as this, so don't be expecting too much."

"I think I can handle it."

"I'm not in any big hurry to get to the Arizona Territory this time o' year," Wiley said.

"Why is that?"

"Well, if you thought it was hot in New Orleans, you ain't seen nothin' yet. We may have to confine ourselves to the northern part of the territory until fall. The south is mostly desert, blistering heat, scorpions, not to mention hostile Apaches, maybe tougher than any of the Plains Indians."

"Why would you want to drag me off to a place like that?" I asked in mock seriousness.

"Excitement, adventure, wealth! To be a part of history! Think of the books you could write! Think of your memoirs!"

"I'm a little young, at thirty-four, to be thinking of my memoirs."

Wiley laughed. "You'd better get 'em done while you're still hale and hearty. If we have nine lives like cats, you and I've been through about seven of 'em already."

A sudden babble of loud voices interrupted him and pulled our attention back to the saloon.

The noise was coming from a small crowd standing around a table about halfway back on the port side. I

14

caught a glimpse of two men who were part of the prince's party.

"What now?"

"Let's go see," Wiley said, picking up his drink.

"Always rushing in where angels fear to tread," I commented dryly. But I followed his lead, and we joined the curious onlookers who were gravitating toward the disturbance. Several well-dressed ladies were in the gathering crowd. We edged our way through until we could see what was happening.

Everyone was standing. The prince, flanked by his four retainers, was facing a man across the table.

"If you can't afford to lose, you shouldn't gamble," the man behind the table was saying calmly as he riffled a pack of cards in his huge hands.

"That was not gambling, sir. That was cheating!" Prince Zarahoff retorted through clenched teeth, his accent very pronounced. The gambler shrugged, nonchalant, but I noticed his eyes darting from one to another of the men facing him for any sign of a weapon.

"That's George Devol," Wiley hissed in my ear, as if the name should mean something to me, but it rang no familiar chord. "Notorious gambler, cheater, and fighter. He's been on this river since I was a kid. I heard my dad talk of him years ago," he whispered in reply to my quizzical look.

The man he spoke of didn't look dangerous, standing there in a neat, black suit and tie and a white shirt. He was a blocky man, about six feet tall, and I guessed he weighed close to 200 pounds. He had black hair and a gray-tinged goatee and mustache that hid his mouth and chin. If the size of his hands was any indication, he was probably as strong as a bear. But he looked to be close to fifty years old.

"If you're not going to play, move on," Devol said shortly. "You're holding up my game."

This seemed to infuriate Prince Zarahoff. The young man's face flushed a deep red. "I demand you return my money this instant, or I shall have you put off this boat at the next landing! In my country, we have men like you shot!"

"We're not in your country now, so move along," Devol replied evenly. He made as if to select the cards for another game of three-card monte, but he was warily watching Prince Ferdinand for any quick moves. "Take your medicine and go," he said. "A short stack of gold pieces is a cheap enough price for a good lesson. Never go up against a professional unless you can afford to lose. And you, obviously, can afford to lose." He indicated the prince's rich clothing and emerald-encrusted ring.

"I *know* I selected the right card," the prince persisted, "I bent the corner of that card myself when you weren't looking."

"Then, obviously, you meant to cheat me," George Devol countered. "I just took advantage of your greed and beat you at your own game."

"Then just return my money and we will call it even," the prince offered, a little calmer himself.

"How do you think I make my living?" Devol almost sneered at him. "It sure as hell isn't by returning the money of every easy mark who comes along."

A smaller man, whom I took to be the gambler's partner and capper, and who had probably set up this little con-game, edged away from Devol and appeared to be tensing up for action. Although I could see no gun on either of them, I felt fairly certain they were both armed.

16

Prince Zarahoff clenched and unclenched his fists as if uncertain what to do next. The small walnut table separated them, and the tightly packed crowd made it impossible for him to reach Devol without leaping across. Ferdinand Zarahoff was about five ten and slim. Even though he was only about half the gambler's age, I had the feeling be would come off much the worse in any rough and tumble fight.

"Give the man his money back."

All heads turned at this new voice from the edge of the crowd. It was the blond stranger from the hurricane deck.

Devol glanced sideways at him and then dismissed the order as not worth his attention.

Thunk!

The young man's fist shot straight out, and Devol staggered back, blood gushing from his nose into his whiskers. There was a collective gasp of surprise from the crowd as people began to fall back out of the way.

"Damn you!" Devol sputtered, regaining his balance and wiping his mustache with one hand. "I don't know who you are, mister, but, if you're lucky, you'll live to regret the day you did that."

He lunged toward the blond stranger.

"Hold it!" The command cracked like a shot over the noise. Devol stopped and the crowd quieted and backed slightly to make way for a short, bewhiskered man in a cutaway coat. "I run a respectable boat here, and I'll have no fighting," he snapped. His face flushed pink. "If you gentlemen have any personal differences to settle, you can do it ashore. We'll be wooding up at Hog Point shortly. If you're still inclined to fight, you can do it there." He glared about him for a few seconds and then turned and pushed his way out of the crowd.

"Who was that?"

"Probably the captain, or one of the owners. They'd be the only ones with that much authority," Wiley replied.

"When the bow of this boat runs ashore, you'd better be ready," the gambler growled, dabbing at his swollen nose with a bloodstained handkerchief. "Or I'll come and get you wherever you may be hiding."

The blond stranger said nothing, but his face seemed to have gone white under his light tan. With one last glance at Devol, he walked away. Devol and his partner picked up their cards and headed for the bar.

"Ten to one on Devol," someone in the crowd cried.

"Make that twenty to one and you've got it," another man answered as the buzzing of the crowd indicated renewed interest in this encounter. A good fight would break the monotony of the trip.

"God, Matt, we can't let that little guy go up against Devol," Wiley said, automatically taking up for the underdog.

"It's none of our business. He dealt himself into this."

"But Devol will kill him."

"No, he won't. If he wants to continue working this river, he'll just rough him up good. Killing a smaller man like that, even in a fair fight, would hurt his reputation, and these boat captains wouldn't be near as ready to wink at the prohibition against gambling."

I could tell from Wiley's face that he was not convinced. I was not really convinced myself, since I didn't know George Devol. But my argument sounded good.

I suddenly remembered Prince Zarahoff and looked around in the milling crowd, but he and his cohort had disappeared in the excitement.

"C'mon. Let's go back to the cabin and change to some more comfortable clothes," I suggested, setting my empty glass on the table. "Even if you're right, there's nothing we can do about it."

"Maybe there is," he replied thoughtfully as we started toward our adjoining staterooms.

Just as we spoke, a slackening in the tempo of the paddle wheels indicated the *Silver Swan* was coming up on Hog Point.

CHAPTER 3

"WHAT HAVE YOU GOT IN MIND?" I ASKED AS WE stripped off our dinner clothes and pulled on some cotton shirts and worn corduroys.

"We've got to find him and hide him somewhere before this boat stops."

"You heard what Devol said—that he'd find him no matter where he was hiding."

"This is a big boat. If we can keep him out of sight long enough for the boat to wood up and get underway, the whole thing may blow over. Devol won't be allowed to do any fighting on board."

"What if the stranger doesn't want to hide?"

Did you see his face when Devol threatened him? He was terrified."

"Well"—I shrugged—"I guess it won't hurt to give it a try. If that young man has been at sea for several years, he probably doesn't know Devol's reputation as a fighter. Let's get out there and see if we can intercept him."

The cabin was still about half-full of people milling around, and there were three tables of men playing cards

19

near the ladies' end of the cabin. We searched the crowd quickly but didn't see the blond stranger.

"What room is his?"

"Don't know. Let's look up the clerk and find out."

"No time. We're stopping." The crowd began to move toward the stairways at either end of the long cabin. Even the women seemed thrilled by the prospect of viewing the bloodletting, discussing it among themselves.

"He may be down on deck," I suggested.

"Or he could have already found himself a hiding place."

"Let's get down on the main deck," I said, feeling a slight bump as the *Silver Swan* nudged up to the bank. The main saloon had nearly emptied.

Just as we started for the forward end, I caught sight of a lone figure moving out between the velvet drapes of an arch near one of the staterooms.

"There he is," I whispered hoarsely to Wiley. We angled over to head him off. He looked up sharply as we accosted him, but then his face relaxed somewhat as he recognized us. He looked even paler than before. I took his arm and pulled him back through one of the curtained archways.

"You're not really going down there to fight him, are you?" Wiley demanded, as if the idea were unthinkable. "He'll beat you to a pulp."

"Lemme alone!" he retorted, jerking his arm free. "I gotta do it."

"Why?" Wiley persisted. "What's it going to prove? You already got in a good lick. And getting yourself beat up sure isn't going to get Prince Zarahoff his money back. What difference does all this make to you, anyway?"

20

"Makes no difference now," he said, moving off. "I started this, and I've got to see it through."

"Why?" Wiley asked again.

He turned his face to us. "Because if I don't, I'll be branded a coward."

"Who cares what other people think?"

"I have to live with myself."

Wiley shook his head, uncomprehending.

"Besides," the young man, continued, walking out into the empty saloon, "this boat isn't big enough to hide me if I don't go down there."

"We could black your face and hands with charcoal, put a hat on you and slip you ashore with the Negro roustabouts while they're handling the wood," Wiley said as a last resort.

"And then what? Lost at night in the middle of some bayou? And not knowing when the next boat is coming along, of if it would put in for a hail? And how do I know what kind of trash may be running that woodyard? No, thanks. I'll take my chances with Devol."

Wiley had run out of arguments. We followed the stranger as he headed toward the stairway; he seemed almost eager to get it over with. The whole thing was a mystery. We didn't even know the blond man's name.

Below, the main deck was like another world. Crowds of deck and cabin passengers were jammed together in a surging mass, most of them crowding toward the one, narrow gangplank that had been thrown across to a bank that was slightly higher than the main deck. Several blazing torches were fastened high overhead to the upper-deck supports, illuminating the human horde in an eerie, flickering light.

21

"Gangway, there! Make room for my men to get ashore. Dammit! If you're not handling wood, get out of the way!"

A man who stood head and shoulders above the crowd was shoving his way out from under the stairs where we stood, knocking people left and right with amazing strength. Although there was hardly room to fall down, several men near the edge of the crowd went sprawling into the starboard guards. At the same time, I heard some yelling and cursing and saw three or four figures fall from the plank to the mud and water a few feet below.

The big mate merged with a swarm of deckhands near the rounded bow. In a matter of seconds he had six men on the tail of a line running through a double block secured to the end of an overhead boom. With this mechanical leverage, they were able to lower the eight-foot-wide, fifty-foot-long landing stage from its upright position across to the sloping shore. No sooner was it in place and braced than it was filled with a moving stream of passengers going ashore. Even so, it was a minute or two before the crowd just below us thinned enough for the three of us to get down the last few steps to the deck.

The mate, a giant of a man I estimated to be at least six foot eight or nine, was striding back and forth, yelling at the roustabouts to get a move on as a line of them jogged in a continuous half shuffle back and forth across the bouncing bridge, like a line of ants, carrying the cordwood aboard and stacking it. I noticed some whites among the woodhaulers—probably immigrant deck passengers who were working their passage, I guessed.

"Hey, kid!" the mate yelled as we passed him going for the gangway. "You the one who's going to fight Devol?"

The blond ignored him and jumped nimbly up onto the gangway between two roustabouts.

With a speed that belied his size, the mate made one long leap and snatched the stranger off the gangway and back onto the deck. "Dammit, I'm *talking* to you," he growled in a voice just loud enough for us to hear. I tensed for the fight I knew was coming, but the mate just eased the sailor to his feet and turned him around as if he weighed nothing. "You'd better listen to me if you know what's good for you," the big man continued, ignoring me and Wiley. He spoke in a low voice directly to the white, upturned face of the young seaman. "I've seen Devol in action before, and there's only one thing you have to look out for: He'll butt you with his head the first chance he gets. Don't laugh. He's ruined the faces and smashed the noses of many bigger and stronger men than you. At least one of 'em died— drove his nose bone right into his brain."

The three of us began to listen intently to the information this obviously well-meaning man was giving the sailor.

"He must have a skull as thick as this stanchion," the big man continued. "Never seems to hurt him. He has a few scars up here on his forehead, but most times he combs his hair down over 'em."

"What's your name?" the blond asked, finally finding his voice.

"John Wells," he replied, thrusting out a hand, "I'm the mate of this here packet, and a damn good one if I do say so myself. Most folks just call me Big John."

"Can't imagine why a skinny little fella like yourself would want to fight Devol, but that ain't none o' my affair. But let me give you a little advice if you're determined to do it. He's not as fast on his feet as he

23

used to be, but he's strong. Don't get in close where he can get a grip on you. That's when he'll butt. He's put down some mighty rough river brawlers with that head o' his, so stay clear of it whatever you do."

"Thanks, John," I replied for all of us.

"If you two are friends of his, you'll hustle him outa here," Wells said to me and Wiley.

I just shook my head and shrugged as I turned to follow the sailor and Wiley. As we approached the far end of the landing stage, I could see the glow of a huge fire beyond the lip of the high mud bank that was still a good fifteen feet above our heads. I grabbed the stranger's arm and halted him. "Hey, mister, at least tell us what your name is."

"Yeah, we'll need to know what to put on your tombstone," Wiley added.

"Staghorn," he replied absently, glancing up the darkened hill at the sound of the rumbling crowd. Some strident laughter rose above the noise.

"Last chance to get away from here," I urged him.

His face was only a lighter spot in the darkness.

"I've got to get this over with!" he rasped, as if goading his own courage. Then, without another word, he turned and began climbing the steep bank behind him.

The crowd noise swelled as a few men on the edge of the mob caught sight of Staghorn.

"Here he is—finally! Give him a hand up."

"Thought he'd shucked out!"

"Guess my bet's safe."

He was shoved from hand to hand into the middle of the circle formed by the crowd. Wiley and I were shut off to the outside as they pressed forward to see the fun. We worked our way around to the other side and, with some powerful elbowing, managed to worm our way in close enough to see, even though those at the inner edge of the circle wouldn't budge. One thing that held the spectators back from pressing in any closer was the heat from the huge fire of logs and brush that flamed up in the middle of the clearing. Even as I looked, a burly, bearded man came forward and threw another armload of short logs onto the blazing pile. A shower of sparks fanned up into the night.

Staghorn stood at the far side of the circle from me, his hands at his sides. I craned my neck around the man in front of me for a glimpse of Devol. I assumed he was in the midst of a knot of friends and supporters to the left of the fire.

"Let's get on with it!" someone near me shouted.

"Yeah. That boat ain't gonna be here forever!"

The crowd broke into cheers and clapping, and I caught sight of Devol, dressed in rough workclothes and moving alone into the circle of light. As he moved forward, he held his arms wide. Staghorn went into a boxer's crouch. Devol looked square and massive compared to the slim sailor. Staghorn was giving away at least three inches in height and a good forty pounds in weight. But he was much younger and apparently quicker.

Devol made a sudden rush, but the blond easily avoided him, chapping a left to the side of his head as the big man went by. The punch connected but didn't faze the gambler. So confident did he appear that he ignored the punches of the younger man and rushed at him, trying to pin him in a bear hug. Again, Staghorn was too quick for him and threw a hard right to the ear just as he spun out of Devol's grip. A piece of Staghorn's shirt ripped away in Devol's clutching hand.

25

The punch stung the gambler, but I noticed Staghorn also wince slightly and open and close his hand several times as he stalled for time by dodging behind the fire.

"Damn!" Wiley burst out. "Why does he keep punching him in the head? Didn't he hear what the mate said?"

Even though Wiley was jammed in next to me, he almost had to shout for me to hear him over the yelling of the mob around us—a mob composed more of cabin passengers with wagering money than with deck passengers. There seemed to be fewer women than I first thought.

Even though Devol was taller, he offered no target other than his head as he came in low. Devol could apparently take any kind of a blow with a fist on his thick skull. I could tell by the yelling that some of the men in the crowd were familiar with Devol's tactics from previous fights—probably the reason that a man nearby shouting that he was giving twenty to one odds, was getting no takers.

The two fighters feinted back and forth on opposite sides of the fire, glaring at each other around the leaping flames, until the crowd started to jeer and whistle and wave for action.

"Get in there and fight, ya damn coward!"

"You're mighty good at slugging somebody when he's not lookin'. What's wrong with ya now?"

"C'mon, mix it up!"

"Go get him, George!"

There was a sheen of sweat on both fighters' faces from the heat of the fire as much as from exertion. The crowd was jammed six deep around the combatants in the sultry air. Staghorn's normally pale face was suffused with color.

Finally, Devol started to his right around the fire, and the lean sailor ran away from him to the jeers of the onlookers. The boos rose to a crescendo as the two men circled the blazing pile. As they went around the second time, I was amazed to see Devol catching up with the nimble Staghorn. The gambler got close and made a grab, but Staghorn suddenly spun and slammed a forearm under the big man's chin, stopping him cold. Devol staggered back, his mouth open, his thick hands going to his windpipe.

The noise of the crowd died in a collective gasp.

Staghorn aimed a kick at Devol's groin. He was slightly off the mark, but close enough to do some damage. While he had the big man reeling, Staghorn slammed a shoulder into him, driving him to the ground, his hands clawing for a chokehold.

"Come on, put him away!" Wiley almost screamed.

But the big man was enormously strong and squirmed just enough to keep Staghorn from forcing his thumbs into his throat. Every second that the sailor was unable to press his advantage was a second Devol was able to recover. I could almost see the pain subsiding and his strength returning. He held his chin tightly to his chest, and I could hear his breath rasping in his throat as he gradually forced his massive forearms up between his body and Staghorn's. Stunned as he was, Devol still fought from instinct, relaxing, recovering, biding his time.

Finally, the gambler gave a convulsive heave, threw Staghorn off, and twisted his big body over on top before the sailor could roll away. The crowd began to shout again. Most of them were siding with the gambler, but a few had taken long odds on the stranger.

Staghorn managed to hit Devol with a short left to the

side of his face as the gambler sat astride him. But then Devol unleashed his infamous weapon. Staghorn saw it coming and twisted his own head to one side at the last instant so that the big man's head caught him only a glancing blow on the left cheekbone. The crowd screamed, sensing the end of the fight.

Even though he was stunned, the sailor apparently sensed he was in deadly danger and managed to struggle over onto his stomach. Devol had relaxed his grip slightly when his own forehead hit the ground after glancing off Staghorn's, cheek. He grabbed Staghorn by the back of his shoulders to try to pry him over, but he couldn't turn the smaller man, who had flattened himself to the ground. Finally, in exasperation, Devol bit down on Staghorn's ear. With a movement so quick I hardly saw it, Staghorn brought his right elbow up in a short, vicious jab. It sank into the gambler's belly, and Devol released his grip with a gasp. The sailor threw him off and was up and away in a second. A kick caught Devol in the side before he could rise. It would have flattened any ordinary man, but Devol was no ordinary man. He could shake off punishment like a grizzly. He got to his feet and rushed at Staghorn, but the younger man was not about to close with him again. He dodged out of the way. Both men were slowing down and panting heavily. They backed away and circled each other cautiously. Devol abandoned his rushing tactics and balled his fists, moving slowly toward Staghorn.

The young sailor's left eye and cheekbone were beginning to discolor. Blood was trickling from his right ear. He ran a sleeve across his face to wipe the sweat from his eyes.

Staghorn danced in and whipped a punch at Devol's head. The big man ducked his head and the fist glanced

28

off harmlessly. Staghorn tried again. Devol staggered slightly and appeared to be hurt. Staghorn moved in to follow up, but the gambler was apparently only decoying. As soon as the sailor was within reach, the big hands grabbed him in a viselike grip. Staghorn realized his mistake instantly and struggled wildly to break free, but to no avail. The gambler brought the battering-ram head into action again and caught the sailor on the corner of the chin. His head snapped back and his eyes glazed. I could see Staghorn's knees buckling, but the bear-hug wouldn't let him fall. Devol aimed another shot with his head, but didn't hit him squarely because the sailor's head was lolling back, almost out of range. I knew it was over, but Devol was enraged and kept slamming his head into the semiconscious Staghorn.

Hardly realizing what I was doing, I shoved my way into the circle, grabbed a smoking stick of firewood from the edge of the pile, and, with one, fast, hard blow, struck the gambler over the right ear. Devol's hold instantly relaxed and both men went crashing to the ground.

A woman in the crowd gave a stifled scream, and a sudden hush fell. I gradually came to myself, standing alone with the smoldering piece of oak in my hand. The next thing I became aware of was a sound, like a low growl, rising from the crowd.

"Who do you think you are, mister?"

Several men moved toward me, menacingly. I turned to face them, keeping the fire at my back, and holding the heavy oak club. Out of the corner of my eye, I could see figures coming around the sides of the fire, closing in. I backed up until the heat stopped me. Strangely enough, I never even thought of reaching for my gun.

Probably just as well, or I would have been a dead man.

"The fight was over, men," I said, trying to keep my voice steady and holding the club in front of me.

"Like hell it was!"

"You son-of-a-bitch! You caused my sure bet to be canceled."

"Throw the meddlin' bastard in the river."

They were in no mood for discussion. I got a better grip on the smoking club and vowed that the first man near me would get the same thing I had given Devol.

CHAPTER 4

MOST OF THE ONLOOKERS WERE HANGING BACK AND watching. Only seven or eight of the drunkest or maddest were coming for me. But that seven or eight might as well have been fifty. One man, in particular, seemed to be the leader. His face was flushed, and his eyes bulged in anticipation as he moved in. His lips curled back in a snarl, and I could see that one of his front teeth was broken off diagonally. I took a deep breath and resolved to take him first. As he came within range, I swung the stick in an arc at his face. He leapt back, and my club caught only the brim of his hat, knocking it flying. I whipped the stick back around, but before I could do any more, two men rushed me from both sides and pinned my arms. The man I had swung at cocked a fist and I braced myself for the blow. The next instant he pitched forward flat on his face at my feet as Wiley Jenkins slammed into his back with a flying tackle. Three men immediately pounced on Wiley with knees and fists.

"Hold on, there!" a giant voice boomed over the melee.

I looked up to see Big John Wells shoving his way into the circle. Nearly everyone fell back to make way for the big man. Nearly everyone, that is, except the three who were pounding Wiley. They jumped up and went for the mate. He disposed of them as he would have a bunch of bothersome curs. Kicking one in the stomach, he grabbed the other two around the necks and brought their heads together with the sound of someone thumping a watermelon. The three went down in a heap. Wells stepped calmy over them and came to me. Even though he wore a big revolver on his hip, he made no move toward it. "You gents want to take your hands off him, or do you need a little persuadin'?"

The two men holding me looked up at his impressive height, glanced at their companions rolling weakly on the ground, and let go of my arms.

He lifted his voice and half turned. "Anybody else hasn't had his fill of fightin', I'll be glad to oblige him."

"And you will kindly take your hand off that gun, or I'll be forced to give you a taste of this fowling piece," a new voice cut in sharply. The dialect was familiar. We all looked around at Prince Ferdinand Zarahoff who stood on the edge of the circle, weapon in hand, pointing it casually in the direction of a well-dressed man about fifteen feet from us. The man's face reddened at this sudden attention, and he slowly withdrew his right hand from under his coat and then ducked out of sight into the crowd.

Before anyone else could move or speak, a blast of the boat's steam whistle startled us. The tension was broken.

"Okay, everyone back aboard!" the mate shouted. "We're gettin' underway!"

The crowd began to break up and disperse.

In the few seconds I had been distracted, the prince had mingled with the crowd of passengers and disappeared as quickly as he had appeared.

"Whew!" I breathed, my heart still pounding. "Big John, you're a lifesaver. Another minute or two and I would have been a battered piece of driftwood."

"We better take a look at your friend over here," the big mate growled, seemingly embarrassed by my gratitude.

Staghorn was sitting up but looking very groggy and feeling gingerly of his face and jaw. His left eye was nearly swollen shut. Devol was being helped away by his partner and two other men.

Big John lifted Staghorn like a rag doll and propped him between Wiley and me. We half walked, half carried him down across the gangway and up the stairs to his stateroom. He was still conscious, but in considerable pain when we stretched him out on his bed. Wiley and I were the only ones there, the only ones who had taken any interest in this stranger. The big mate had stayed below to supervise the casting off. I could feel the vibrations as the engineer reversed the engines and backed the big side-wheeler into midstream.

"Better fetch some water," I told Wiley, handing him the pitcher from the washstand. "And while you're at it, go by the bar and get a bottle; we'll need some disinfectant. I don't think he's got any cuts that'll require stitching. Even if he did, it wouldn't matter; there are no doctors aboard that I know of."

As soon as Wiley closed the door, I pulled off the sailor's shoes and then gently rolled him over and helped him slip out of his shirt that was mostly rags, dirt, and blood. Then he eased back onto the pillow with a sigh and closed his eyes. The adrenaline was not

32

pumping now. The stiffness and the pain were beginning to set in.

"You sure nothing's broken? What about your jaw?"

"Naw," he mumbled through puffy lips. "I'm all right."

He opened his eyes, or rather, one eye. The left one was now swollen shut. He attempted a grin. "Takes more batterin' than that to put me away. Got banged up pretty good one time off the Cape of Good Hope. Big wave fell aboard and washed me off the lifelines into the scuppers. Didn't break anything, but was sore as a boil for a week."

I began a more careful examination of his injuries. Other than a lot of scrapes and scratches, the most severe seemed to be the knot on his jaw and the left cheekbone that was discolored and swollen. The bite on his right ear had clotted but would have to be cleaned thoroughly. I touched his cheekbone below the closed eye and he winced.

"It could be cracked or broken, but it doesn't seem to be out of place. It'll probably heal all right."

The door to the saloon opened and closed quickly behind me. Wiley was back with the water, two fresh towels, a bottle of whiskey, and three glasses.

He splashed some water into the bowl, dipped one of the towels and began cleaning the fighter up. The young man gritted his teeth as we sponged his cuts with the raw whiskey.

"By the way, what's your full name?" Wiley asked him as he worked.

"I told you—Staghorn."

"Staghorn? That's it? You have only one name?"

"Fin Staghorn."

"Finn? Is that a family name?"

33

In spite of his discomfort he seemed embarrassed. "No. It's short for Phineas. But I'd better not hear either of you call me that."

"Okay by me," Wiley said.

"Fin it is," I agreed, trying to suppress a smile.

"Father's English, mother's Norwegian," he continued. "They both came over when they were in their teens. Met and married in Iowa. I was born in Minnesota."

There came a soft knock at the door leading to the outside deck. Wiley and I jumped and the three of us looked at each other.

"You expecting someone?"

Staghorn silently shook his head. He and Wiley were not armed, so I put my hand on my holstered Colt and motioned for Wiley to open the door. The door swung out and Prince Zarahoff stood framed in the light.

We were so taken aback that no one said a word for a few seconds while the prince stood there, obviously awaiting an invitation to enter. Finally, our visitor spoke. "Are these the accommodations of the young man who just fought the gambler?"

"Yes . . ." I said, finally finding my voice. "Yes. Come in." He appeared to be alone.

Staghorn nodded his assent from his bed without attempting to speak through his swollen lips.

The lean, dark-haired man stepped inside, and Wiley closed the door. The churning of the big paddle wheel and the puffing of escaping steam could still be heard through the open transom.

"I came to thank you for what you did," the prince began, addressing the sailor who had propped himself up on one elbow. "You Americans are an unusual people. I don't even know your name. I am Ferdinand Zarahoff of Rumania."

34

He didn't offer to shake hands.

"Fin Staghorn," the sailor replied. "Nice to make your acquaintance, Prince."

"Please do not use my title," the prince said. "While I am a visitor in your country, I wish to drop all references to my royalty. I came here to experience the American Wild West, and I want to be treated as any other citizen of your country."

"Not likely," Wiley said, glancing at the yellow silk shirt Prince Ferdinand was wearing. "Where are your tough-looking buddies?"

Zarahoff's mouth compressed into a thin line under his mustache and he shot a hard look at Wiley Jenkins. It was the look of a man who is not used to having his statements questioned.

"I came to say thank-you," Zarahoff continued. He turned and spoke to Staghorn. "I admire men with courage such as you have. I don't know what your motive was. However, I would like to invite you to join my entourage. You could function as my personal bodyguard and advise me on American customs."

He spoke excellent English with a pronounced British accent. He had undoubtedly been schooled in the safety of an English environment—probably while Rumania was in the turmoil of revolution.

"Of course, I have engaged your famous frontiersman, Buffalo Bill Cody, as host and guide for my western tour. But I could use a man like you."

"Thanks, Prince," Fin managed a crooked smile through his swollen lips. "But I quit the sea because I'm tired of being another man's lackey. I've got plans of my own."

"Well, that is unfortunate. Are all Americans as independent as you?" He shook his head. "It appears I

35

have much to learn about the character of the unschooled backwoodsman. In case you should change your mind . . ." He left the offer hanging. "Good evening, gentlemen." He made a slight bow and let himself out.

Staghorn's face had clouded. " 'Unschooled back-woodsman'? Who the hell does he think he is?"

"An egotistical prince who has power and money," I grinned.

"Should have asked him how much he was paying," Wiley said, splashing a little whiskey into one of the glasses and adding some water. "You really got something better to do?" he asked, handing the glass to Fin.

"No. Just want to get home. Haven't seen my folks in a couple of years. They're trying to make a go of homesteading in eastern Dakota. My dad's not as young as he used to be. Thought maybe I'd give 'em a hand—get my feet on solid ground again. Then I'll decide what I want to do."

Wiley took a seat on the end of the bed since I was using the tiny stateroom's only chair.

"Hand me a shirt out of that seabag," Fin said. As he pointed to his duffle in the corner, I noticed for the first time the skinned and swollen knuckles. Wells had been right about Devol's head being as hard as a battering ram. Staghorn was lucky to have come away with no damage to his nose or teeth, and apparently without a concussion.

"I don't remember introducing myself to you," I said as Wiley was helping him gingerly into a clean cotton shirt. "Even if you're not interested, I'm Matthew Tierney, and this is Wiley Jenkins. I don't know how we got mixed up in all this. But if Wiley hadn't been so

36

nosy, you'd very likely have been killed or crippled."

"Sorry," he mumbled. "Thanks for all your help. Guess I was just too busy to be grateful." He thrust out his hand.

"I would still like to know whatever possessed you to slug Devol in the first place," I said, gripping his hand lightly.

"I don't know as I can really explain it myself," he mused, lying back against the headboard and staring ahead at nothing. "I guess I've always had a feeling for the underdog, and that poor sucker just seemed like the underdog at the time."

"Huh!" I snorted. "He had three or four musclemen with him. And he could probably buy and sell a half-dozen boats like this, and fire everybody on them."

"Well, I don't know. Maybe it wasn't exactly that. I think it sort of scared me, too."

"Why? You weren't involved."

"Not directly. But it's just the idea that if Devol could do that to someone as powerful as that prince—and him a visitor in this country—he could do it to anyone."

"But they were both trying to cheat," I persisted. "Even though, I'll admit, Devol was the professional at it."

He didn't reply for a few seconds. He sipped his drink and stared vacantly at the coal-oil lamp in its brass sconce on the outboard bulkhead. The silence stretched out, and I began to believe that he had abandoned the discussion altogether. Finally he spoke in a voice so low I thought for a second he was talking to himself. "Ever since, I was a little kid, I've been a coward," he said. It was obviously a very painful admission. "Oh, I did a lot of foolish and dangerous things, like most boys do, but I was a coward when it came to other people and other

37

kids at school. It wasn't just boys bigger than I was, either. But you know how boys are. When they found out I was scared of any kind of physical combat, they went after me. I was constantly running from fights, or begging for mercy if one of them got me on the ground. It pains me to think of it now. I was ridiculed and laughed at and called names. They made fun of my name, Phineas, and I've been sensitive about it ever since."

I started to say something, but thought it best not to break in on his train of thought. He stared ahead at nothing, his thoughts probing deep within himself and his past.

"It finally reached a point where I knew I was going to have to run or stand and defend myself," he continued. "I guess I was just afraid of physical injury. I was small for my age, but quick, so running seemed better than fighting—fighting I saw no purpose in. Why get bloodied up or have your teeth broken over some stupid argument, or to prove you're not chicken? It became a favorite sport of some of the bigger boys to pick a fight with me at recess every day, just to see me run or cringe."

He paused again to sip his drink. The air was becoming close in the tiny room and perspiration was forming on his forehead, but I made no move to open either door.

"Well, one day the school bully—Stacey MacDougall was his name—started his regular routine of taunting me in the schoolyard. But he made the mistake that day of slapping me in the face. And something snapped inside me. I tore into him with fists flying. He was fifteen years old and I was barely thirteen at the time, and he outweighed me a good thirty pounds, but I didn't care. I was mad. I took him by surprise and got in a few good punches. Then he proceeded to beat the hell out of me. Gave me a bloody nose, split my lip, tore my clothes. But, in spite of it all, I was glad I did it. Some of my classmates secretly congratulated me on standing up to MacDougall. I caught more hell at home for ripping up my clothes than I did for fighting, since my mom had to make most of my clothes, and I had two younger sisters she had to sew for, too. But that was a turning point for me. Nobody bothered me at school after that. I even seemed to gain a little respect, and was included in their ball games and such. But it didn't cure me of being afraid. I was just as scared as I ever was. So I made up my mind that the only way to overcome fear was to push it aside and go after whatever it is that's scaring you. And that's the course I've followed ever since."

He licked his dry lips and took another sip of the watered whiskey, grimacing slightly, either at the taste or the sting of the alcohol on the cuts inside his mouth.

"We had a span of mean, biting and kicking mules on the farm," he went on, "and I purposely asked my dad if I could harness them up and try to drive them. I was scared to death at first, but gradually I was able to handle them by myself.

"After I left school, I read a lot—mostly thrillers or dime novels. Also read a lot about the sea, even though I had never seen the ocean. My head got full of all those romantic notions of adventure on the high seas and such, you know . . . So, anyway, at eighteen, I left the farm, with my folks' reluctant blessing, and headed toward the nearest port at New Orleans to sign on a deepwater voyage. Came down to the gulf by steamboat. Cheaper and easier than going overland to the East Coast.

"But when I got there and talked to some of the sailors and saw what it was really like, that old fear began to come back. The more I realized what was ahead of me as a totally inexperienced hand before the mast, the more afraid I got. I walked along the dock and looked at those magnificent tall ships, and was thrilled. But then I heard tales of cruelty and hardship from the sailors off those ships, and I cringed. To them it was all in a day's work, but I was so scared, I shook. But I was determined to go through with it. Besides, I had no money to go home; my father had paid my passage, and I was ashamed to go home. Everyone was looking for hands then, so it was no problem finding a berth, even for an inexperienced hand like me who didn't know a halyard from a mooring line.

"To make a long story short, I've just finished my fifth voyage in six years. And I can tell you I found a life I had reason to fear. It's mostly hard, dangerous, and low-paid. Cold, wet work day and night for weeks on end with little food and little rest. I never really got used to going aloft in a blow to handle sail, but I managed to fight down my fear and do it. I had no choice. But I think I'm a better man for it now," he said proudly. "I wouldn't trade my experience for anything."

He sighed, set his glass down, and laid his head back on the pillow, closing his eyes for a few seconds. It was quite a speech, I thought, for a man with a cut and swollen mouth who was having to form his words carefully—but a speech I sensed he had to make.

"Saved up the money from my last voyage to buy cabin passage home," Staghorn went on after a moment. "It was a hard trip around the Horn from California. Snow and hail and nothing but gales through the roaring forties. Swore I'd sleep in every time the watches changed on this packet. Eat and sleep to my heart's content. . ." His voice trailed off as he closed his eyes again. Then he roused himself and forced himself to continue as if he had not gotten to the point of his story. "Didn't mean to bore you with my life story. But you kept asking why I slugged Devol. I did it because I was scared of him. I did it because I've trained myself to attack anything that frightens me. It was as much a reflex as whacking the head of a buzzing rattlesnake."

"I'm surprised you've lived to be as old as you are," I remarked. "That kind of a reflex can have disastrous results."

"Maybe so," he nodded, "but I'd never go back to running from things that scare me."

"Well, maybe things will level off for you someday," I said, getting up and laying a hand on his shoulder. "Someday you'll learn to use that fear in a controlled way—with a sprinkling of judgment. Fear isn't always a bad thing—it can be nature's way of warning us. And running isn't always a sign of cowardice."

He started to retort, but I cut him off by motioning to Wiley. "Come on, let's let him get some rest; he's earned it."

I turned as we went out the door to the promenade deck. "If it's any comfort, we're behind you all the way. If you need anything, or if anyone bothers you, we're in cabin sixteen, just two doors back. I don't think anybody will bother you tonight. Do you have a gun, just in case?"

"No."

"Here." I slipped my Colt out and tossed it onto his bed. "Put that under your pillow. It's loaded. We'll see you in the morning." I closed the door before he could reply.

Wiley and I walked a few steps down the deck before I spoke. "Quite a character. How old would you say he is?"

"Oh, probably two or three years younger than I am—I'd say twenty-five or twenty-six. Feisty little gamecock, isn't he?"

"Sure is."

Wiley patted his pockets. "Damn! Left my cigars in the room. Oh. well, maybe I've been smoking too much lately anyway."

"Yeah. Your lungs are gonna look like the inside of one o' these fireboxes if you don't ease up."

I stared down at the row of reflected lights in the black water that slid along the side of the big boat. Outside our floating world of light and human activity, the unseen woods were creeping past.

I took a deep breath of the soft night air and felt the tension begin to drain away. The air had a fresh, moist smell. I paused at the rail and glanced at the sky from under the deck overhang. A breeze had sprung up, and the moon and stars were obscured by clouds. Even as I stared into the blackness, I felt a drop or two of rain hit my face. It would be a good night for sleeping, I thought, if we could get some of that breeze into our rooms.

"What time is it?" I asked Wiley. "I left my watch in the stateroom."

"Don't know. So much has happened since supper, it feels like it ought to be midnight. But I'd guess about ten."

"I'm going to take a stroll around the boat before I go to bed."

"I'll join you. I need to unwind. I'm not sleepy yet."

We strolled aft on the port side to where the pantry

blocked the sweep of deck and then climbed the stairs to the hurricane deck to continue our walk.

As we passed the housing of the port-side paddle wheel, I noticed that the tempo of the paddle had slowed. Navigating at night must be very difficult, even on a river of this size, I thought. I wondered why the boat didn't tie up at night, especially on a night with no moon or stars to help the pilot get his bearings.

The creaking, groaning, and throbbing of the machinery, along with the explosive puffs of steam escaping through the tall pipes nearby, prevented any conversation for the moment.

While my mind was on the navigation of the steamer, I was startled by two figures darting out of the shadows of the wheelhousing almost at my elbow. They ran forward up the sloping deck toward the stern. There were the sounds of a scuffle in the darkness, then a yell, stifled quickly.

"C'mon, Wiley!" I sprinted toward the fight. But a sudden scream told me it was too late. I saw a form go over the low rail toward the river.

"Man overboard! Man overboard!" Wiley was yelling as we ran. The two dark figures were sprinting around the curve of hurricane deck.

"Get up to the pilothouse!" I shouted at Wiley. "Tell 'em to stop engines. I'll go after them!"

Wiley disappeared and I lunged up the sloping deck, angling toward the starboard side, trying to keep my eyes fixed on the spot where the two running figures had vanished.

As I rounded the Texas on the dead run, something slammed into my stomach, and lights exploded before my eyes as I pitched forward and went sliding down the deck. In a flash I realized my mistake, but it was too late.

43

CHAPTER 5

THE PAIN WAS INTENSE. MY BREATHING WAS paralyzed. Hands and legs were pinning me to the wooden deck, but I couldn't have moved, regardless. I could hear voices as someone struggled to lift me, but, in my daze of pain, I couldn't understand what was said. Through the fog in my brain, a bell was clanging and someone was shouting in the distance. My mouth was open and gasping, but no sound came out. I was being swung by my hands and feet. Then I felt my body being hurled into the air. There was a sickening sensation of falling as I hurtled down and down. I instinctively twisted around, arms in front of my face, not knowing what I would hit.

I slammed into the river on my head and shoulder, and the concussion jerked my neck as I plunged down deep into the sudden silence, holding my breath. The shock of the cool water partially cleared my senses, and I fought and clawed for the surface. My head and arms popped out and I was finally able to suck in a deep lungful of precious air. I wiped the water from my eyes, and there were the lights of the *Silver Swan*, about thirty yards off and moving slowly away from me. I could hear the wheels still churning the black water, but they were slowing.

I took another deep breath and began yelling for help at the top of my voice. Every deep breath hurt my stomach muscles, but I didn't care. At least I was alive. I couldn't tell how far my shouts carried but could see a few running figures on the boiler deck as they passed the lights of open doorways.

I paused for breath, and I could hear some shouted

orders but could not make out the words. The paddle wheels slowed still further, until they were barely holding the big boat against the current. I thought the boat was still moving forward, since it was gradually retreating from me, but then I realized with a shock that I was drifting downstream, away from the boat.

Another man had been pitched off the opposite side of the hurricane deck at the stern shortly before I was hit and thrown overboard. I didn't know who he was or if he was living or dead.

I could see torches being carried along the main deck, and then I heard the booming voice of Big John Wells ordering the deck hands to get a boat over the side. Apparently the big yawls slung in davits outboard of the rail on the boiler deck were used only when the steamboat was in danger of sinking. Smaller skiffs were below on the main deck for such workaday chores as hauling lines ashore, taking soundings, or rescuing drowning passengers. Except for the slow churning of the paddle wheels, and the hooting of an owl somewhere in the trees along the shore, it was a quiet night. I could hear a boat being lowered with a lot of fumbling and bumping, and the voice of Big John Wells cursing the clumsy slowness of the deckhands.

Finally the boat splashed into the water, and the men tumbled in. I could see a torch being handed down to the man in the stern. Then came the sound of oars working in oarlocks, and the light of the torch moved away from the *Silver Swan*. The coxswain was holding the torch high, illuminating his own boat and a large circle of water around it, but I was sure he could see nothing beyond that. I had been treading water, letting the big Mississippi swirl me along, but only when I tried a sidestroke upstream did I realize the force of the current. I was making no progress at all, and the lights of the boat were gradually receding. I felt a moment of panic. Maybe the men in the boat wouldn't see me, I thought. I paused in my swimming and began yelling once more.

The *Silver Swan* had apparently been in a crossing on a bend from the lee of one slack-water shore to the other when I went overboard somewhere in mid-channel. I had no idea how wide the river was at this point. All I knew was that I was treading water and being carried rapidly away from help. I yelled again, and then again.

"Okay, mister, we're comin' t'get ya. Hang on," a deep voice from the boat answered.

"Keep talking so we can find you," another voice said. The man at the tiller held the torch higher, illuminating the three men in the boat as the oarsmen pulled toward me.

I guided them with my voice, and within a minute or two, the boat was alongside and I was being pulled up and in. I fell into the bottom, streaming water.

"Thanks," I managed to gasp, holding my bruised stomach muscles. "Somebody . . . got thrown off . . . the port side . . . just before I . . ."

"What? There's another one?"

"We were told there was only one."

"I didn't hear nobody but you," the first man said.

"Hell, he was hollerin' so much, we couldn't a'heard nobody else."

I sat up, my back to the bow, and wiped the water from my face. I was overcome with gratitude at being alive and safe with little or no damage.

"You men in the boat—over here!"

The call came to us clear and calm across the water. There was no trace of panic or fear. In fact, it verged on

46

sounding like a command rather than a request.

The three deckhands looked at each other. "Who was that?"

"Where are you?" the man with the torch yelled.

"Over here," the voice replied promptly. "Toward the left shore and downstream a little."

With a jolt I recognized the voice as that of Prince Ferdinand Zarahoff!

The men took up their oars and began pulling hard toward the sound. Every few seconds, at the coxswain's instructions, the prince would say something to keep them on course. We passed below the looming bulk of the *Silver Swan* and then drew slowly away from it as the men put their backs into their rowing. Since it was so dark it was almost impossible to tell how fast we were making leeway downstream. We appeared to be standing in one spot, while the voice moved around. The men were trying to get above the voice and then drift down to him. And they succeeded—barely.

"Over here." The voice sounded only a few yards away. The man at the tiller turned us downstream toward the sound, and the men pulled one sweep when the boat suddenly went aground. All three of them were thrown off the thwarts at the sudden stop. The torch went flying and rolled up the sloping sand bar.

The soggy figure of Prince Zarahoff stepped into the light of the still guttering torch and picked it up.

"It's about time, gentlemen," he said, climbing over the side and seating himself near me in the bow as the deckhands untangled themselves. "I was beginning to think I would have to spend the night on this wretched sand spit." He held up the torch and looked around. "Ah, we keep running into each other, Mr . . . ?"

47

"Tierney. Matthew Tierney," I replied, somewhat flabbergasted at his casual attitude. He acted as if he had just been inconvenienced, rather than nearly drowned. The deckhands sensed his condescending attitude but apparently were a little awed in the presence of royalty.

"Give 'er a shove off," the helmsman directed me. I got out and put my shoulder to the stempost. Churning my boots in the soft, wet sand, I broke the boat free, then threw myself across the bow as it swung clear.

"C'mon, back water and pull 'er about," the man at the tiller growled. "Let's get aboard before the *Swan* drifts back and piles the whole kit and caboodle up on this bar."

It was an hour later. After a joyous reunion with Wiley and Fin, I changed into dry clothes and was headed through the grand saloon when I spotted Prince Ferdinand sitting alone at a table.

"May I join you?"

He glanced up with a look of interest in his brown eyes and motioned silently at an empty chair opposite him. "Sit." There was a drink on the table, and I suspected it was not his first.

"Will you have some refreshment?"

I didn't really want anything to drink, but to have an excuse for staying, I nodded. He signaled a white-coated waiter who was still on duty near the bar, and I ordered a whiskey.

"I favor vodka, myself," he said slowly, tipping up his glass. "A taste acquired from my father, I'm afraid."

"The name Zarahoff is Russian?" I ventured.

"Yes. I was born in Rumania, but my mother was English, a kinswoman of Queen Victoria, and my father is Russian. His mother—my grandmother—was a German girl of the Hohenzollern family. Naturally, I

48

grew up speaking English and Russian, as well as learning Rumanian from the servants and my tutors."

"How did your folks wind up in Rumania?" I asked. I felt rather foolish referring to the king and queen of Rumania as "folks," but I wanted to know more about this man whose life had become intertwined with mine during the last twenty-four hours. I could tell from his friendlier, less formal demeanor that our shared experience in the dark, swift waters of the Mississippi was an unspoken bond between us. But then, it may have been the vodka.

"It's quite a long story. Are you really interested, or are you just making conversation?" The friendly smile belied the bluntness of his words.

"I asked, didn't I?"

"Then I must give you some background." He took a deep breath and appeared to be collecting his thoughts. I sipped my whiskey and waited.

"I don't know if you are familiar with the history of my country, but the land was settled, as far back as anyone knows, by barbaric tribesmen before the time of Christ. Later, the area was conquered by soldiers of the Roman Empire. Over the course of many centuries, the region evolved into several individual principalities— Transylvania, Moldavia, Walachia, among others. The whole region has been fought over for centuries. The Turks had it for a long time, and in the last century, they turned over the governing of the various principalities to some wealthy Greeks from Constantinople."

He paused and glanced sharply at me. "You're sure I'm not boring you?"

"Not at all."

"Well, these Greeks proved to be terrible masters. They treated the peasants very harshly and taxed them more heavily than ever. The peasants suffered horribly, then finally revolted in 1821 and forced the Turks to remove the Greek rulers. Russia and the Ottoman Empire have been warring for centuries, and in the decades that followed, the Russians gradually forced the Turks out. A movement to unify the principalities was growing, but there was no agreement on how it should be done. Finally, the wealthy landowners agreed to select a neutral ruler from one of the royal families of Europe. My father, a young Russian prince, was chosen. Shortly after he arrived in Rumania he married my mother, whom he had been courting for some time." He paused and took a swallow of his vodka and stared down at the table for a moment or two. "I don't know whether it was because my father had such responsibility thrust upon him at an early age, or whether it was just his own peculiar personality, but he became very serious. At least since I've been old enough to understand, he has never laughed or joked. He permits no levity or lighthearted fun in the palace. The only parties that took place in our palace in Bucharest were strictly affairs of state, staged only out of duty, and for political contacts. It was all very drab. I seldom got a chance to meet any friends my own age. My father hated the palace at Bucharest and had a small castle in the mountains, mainly for a summer retreat."

As the liquor loosened the tongue of this young visitor, I marveled at the world, so different from my own, that he was revealing. He spoke of palaces and castles as places where people actually lived their daily lives, much as I might refer to a clapboard cottage or a log house.

"The mountain castle was my favorite, too, but I still had little freedom to wander the woods outside in summer. I was forced by protocol to attend interminable meetings and discussions that were full of politics and intrigue . . . Ugh!" He took another drink. "If there be such a disease as terminal boredom, I'm sure I was exposed to it." He smiled ruefully. "You may think the life of a prince is luxury and idleness with every wish fulfilled. Far from it. True, I had every creature comfort I could wish for, but I had virtually no freedom to come and go. It was like living in a luxurious prison. I was taught to ride, and was given lessons in handling small arms, and classes in military tactics—which I detested. I accompanied my uncles on hunting trips in the mountains when they happened to come and visit. But I am an only son, and my father was fearful that something might happen to me and I would not be able to succeed him. Actually, I've been thinking of some way to abdicate without breaking his heart. I just don't have the stomach or the devious mind for international intrigue. I believe I could rule a well-ordered and civilized country, but Rumania has been in turmoil for centuries. In spite of some land reforms instituted by my father, the peasant farmers are still in dire poverty. The wealthy landowners are, I believe, plotting to overthrow the monarchy and install some form of representative government—with some of their own at the head of it, of course, The national treasury is nearing depletion due to the cost of the first Rumanian railroad my father is trying to get built."

"Whew! It's no wonder the king is a somber man, with all that on his back." I leaned back in my chair and crossed my legs.

"Ah, but that is not all. When I left, the Russians had declared war on Turkey and were massing troops to march down from the north. This is nothing new; they have been at war off and on for years, but the fighting this time may very well take place in the middle of Rumania. My father is in a very ticklish position. He must declare our allegiance to one side or the other, or try to maintain some position of neutrality. He is Russian, so it will be difficult, no matter what he does. If he throws Rumania on the side of the Russians, he will have to furnish troops for the cause. I was agitating for a place as an officer with our own troops when my father decided that this might be a good time for me to take the trip to America I had dreamed of for so long. The American West has always fascinated me. When I was a boy I read everything I could get my hands on about the West. So I jumped at the chance to come here, even though I knew he was just trying to get me out of the country for a while. He arranged, through your government, for me to be escorted on a buffalo hunt by your famous Buffalo Bill Cody. I guess my father thought America was a safe place."

"It hasn't been too safe so far. You were very lucky to survive that episode earlier tonight. I wonder who could have done it?"

"Someone playing a practical joke, I presume," he replied with a slight shrug. "Someone wanting to see me embarrassed."

"Practical joke? I think someone was trying to kill you. And, when I tried to stop them, they also tried to kill me."

"I hardly think so. Just some sort of rough frontier humor. Nothing more. Even so, I wish your young friend had accepted my offer. I'd like to have an American guide. My four men are good and loyal, but they, like me, are unfamiliar with this country, its people and customs."

"Where are your men, by the way?"

"They've retired now that they know I'm safe."

I leaned forward, sipping my whiskey thoughtfully and gazing at the emerald and ruby by rings on the prince's hands.

"It might be a good idea," I suggested hesitantly, "to put away your rings and your silk shirts and begin dressing more like an American. Don't flaunt your wealth among these people. You will attract enough attention as it is."

"Perhaps. But I have lived in a cocoon all my life. If I can't let down and enjoy myself here in America, where and when will I ever be able to?"

Thinking of the heavy responsibilities that awaited him, I had no answer. "Just be a little cautious," I said, rising from the table and turning up my glass. "And now I must be going. If you'll excuse me, I'll say good night."

He raised his glass in a half salute, and a smile stretched the corners of his heavy black mustache.

As I walked away, I wondered if I had been privileged to see a part of this unique and lonely man that few others would ever see. I was convinced that someone had tried to kill him. In spite of the fact, that he had made light of the matter, I wasn't convinced that he didn't believe it, too, vodka or no vodka.

It was nearly midnight when I finally stretched my weary frame on the narrow bed in my stateroom. The muscles of my abdomen were still complaining every time I moved.

"You're a mighty lucky man," Wiley said, draping my wet corduroy pants across two wooden pegs on the wall.

"Luck had nothing to do with it," I replied, taking a deep breath and trying to relax. "It was Divine Providence all the way."

"Oh, is that so?" he said, lifting his eyebrows at me. "If I were you, I wouldn't push my luck with the Almighty. It would take both hands to count the potentially fatal scrapes He's gotten you out of just since I've known you. Twice since suppertime you could've easily cashed in your chips."

I chuckled ruefully. "You may be right. You're a bad influence on me. I used to be able to mind my own business and stay out of trouble."

"So, now it's me, is it?" he asked in his best offended manner.

I laughed outright, paining my stomach muscles. "Okay. Okay. You win. If anybody can lay claim to a wee bit of Irish luck, it's Prince Ferdinand Zarahoff of Rumania."

"He's hardly Irish."

"I know. Maybe it's the luck of royalty. First he gets someone to fight his battle for him without even asking, then he gets thrown overboard at night in the middle of a big river, manages to miss anything solid on the way down, and accidentally swims to a high-and-dry sandbar—maybe the only one around—and is picked up inside of twenty minutes. Now, *that's* what I'd call lucky."

"Maybe not so lucky. While he was taking a swim, his stateroom was ransacked."

"What? Any idea who did it?"

"If Captain Wilson has any suspicions, he's not saying. Could've been most anybody. The word was out right away that the royal visitor was overboard."

"Where were his four friends?"

"I was pretty worried about you at the time, but I remember catching sight of one or two of them down on the main deck while Big John was trying to get the boat into the water."

"If the other passengers knew his room was unguarded, somebody took advantage of all the excitement to bust in and steal his money. He shouldn't have been flashing it around that way. Could've been those men who attacked me for breaking up the fight, or it could've been Devol and his partner."

Wiley nodded as he peeled off his shirt and prepared to retire to his adjoining room. "We'll probably never know. The door was unlocked, so they didn't even have to force it. If the prince has any sense, he had his valuables and cash locked up in Captain Wilson's safe. He's not saying if anything's missing."

Wiley, stripped to his shorts, turned up the coal-oil lamp and climbed into the narrow bed in his adjoining room. He pulled the single sheet up to his waist, preparing to read a recent copy of *Harper's Weekly* he had picked up somewhere. But I was still too keyed up to let him do that. The events of the past few hours were whirling in my mind.

"Why would anyone want to throw the prince overboard?" I wondered aloud. "If we hadn't happened along, he could have been killed or marooned on that sand bar. Somebody certainly meant for him to die. A man in the water at the stern of this boat couldn't have made enough noise to attract attention over the sound of the machinery."

"Probably some of Devol's crowd," Wiley guessed, flipping idly through the pages of his magazine. "Still sore about Devol being exposed as a cheat."

"I don't think so. From what I've heard, Devol has

run into plenty of disgruntled customers before. And he's had plenty of fights. But, just from what I've overheard among the passengers, he's never killed anybody."

"Maybe they don't know about any dissatisfied losers who might have mysteriously disappeared," Wiley countered.

"Well, I guess we'll never know for sure," I sighed, picking up one of my soggy boots from beside the bed and pouring a tiny stream of water out of it. "If I hadn't been wearing these short, light boots, I might have drowned, myself. Hope they aren't ruined," I added. "I just bought them last week in New Orleans. Most comfortable cowhide footwear I've ever owned."

"After they dry out in a day or so, oil 'em up good and they should be okay, if the stitching doesn't break."

"Hey, I don't feel the engines vibrating. Why aren't we getting underway again?"

"After you and the prince told your stories to the captain, he gave orders to the pilothouse to bring her into shore and tie up for the night. Too dark and overcast to run safely, what with snags and bars to rip the bottom out of her. While you were having a drink, I went below and talked to the mate. He told me we were tied up on the inside of a big, wooded bend. Any down bound boats that may be running will sweep the bends, so we're safe. We're showing plenty of lights."

"I thought the government was putting up navigation lights on the lower Mississippi."

"They are, but there aren't many of them in place yet. I don't think some of these old-time helmsmen trust them anyway. They'd rather rely on their own experience and instincts."

"And I thought this cruise was going to be a relaxing

56

bit of floating luxury to wind up our vacation," I sighed. "If I'd known what was going to happen inside the first twenty-four hours, I think I'd have taken the train or a stage."

"Well, just sleep late tomorrow morning and forget all about it," Wiley Jenkins advised. "When you get up we'll start fresh. All this will seem like a bad dream."

"With Devol and Staghorn aboard, the memory will be real enough."

"Maybe so," Wiley laughed, "but it's amazing how different things can look in the daylight when you're rested."

"You're right," I conceded, finishing the brandy I had been sipping and setting the glass on the washstand before sliding down in bed and adjusting my pillow comfortably.

CHAPTER 6

BUT MY MUCH-NEEDED REST DIDN'T COME QUICKLY OR easily. My subconscious mind must have stayed alert and on guard, in spite of the brandy I had drunk in hopes of relaxing. I tossed and turned, coming partially awake at one time to see the lamp still burning in the adjoining room and Wiley gone. Sometime later, in the early morning hours, I was vaguely aware of his coming in and going to bed. When I finally did fall into a deep sleep, it lasted until well after sunrise. I heard nothing when the boat backed away from her moorings on the riverbank at dawn and began churning upstream again for Saint Louis.

I finally roused myself when the door banged open from the outside deck and Wiley breezed in, whistling noisily. The cabin was getting uncomfortably warm, and I had kicked the single sheet off in my sleep. Even so, the sultry heat and my deep sleep made me feel drugged. I sat on the side of the bed and held my head in both hands.

"Well, aren't you a sight!" he greeted me cheerily.

I grunted a reply, staggered to a mirror on the bulkhead, and looked at my puffy eyes and my hair sticking out in all directions.

"You missed breakfast," he informed me. "But there's a big table out in the main cabin just piled high with fruit, tarts, and you-name-it."

"I could use some coffee," I replied, pouring water into the china basin and splashing some of it on my face.

"Fine. I'll wait outside. It's a beautiful, sunny day."

He went out, closing the door. I used the slop jar, pulled on some dry, clean clothes, and combed my hair. The machinery throbbed steadily under my feet, and the earthy, fragrant smell of fresh air wafted in through the open transom. Wiley had been right. As I came more fully awake, I felt much better and more rested. I had a feeling that today was going to be a much better day.

I stepped out to join Wiley and took in the glorious sight of the big river sliding by, a seemingly uninterrupted wall of solid forest forming the left side of the Mississippi. I inhaled deeply. I couldn't seem to get enough of the fresh air.

We adjourned into the main saloon to a white-covered table of fruits and sweets, topped by a giant, ornate silver urn of coffee. The coffee smelled delicious, and I drew off a cup. Wiley was eyeing a pretty, dark-haired girl on the opposite side of the table.

"You must not have gotten much sleep last night," I observed, sipping the scalding brew.

"I wasn't really sleepy," he replied absently, catching the eye of the girl across the table and smiling at her as she moved away with an older couple. She noticed Wiley, and nodded pleasantly but did not return the smile. "But you know I'm more, of a night person," Wiley continued.

"Where'd you go?" I asked when I got his attention again.

"Oh, just wandered around. Watched a little poker being played out here."

"Was Devol back in business?"

"Nope. Even though he won that fight, I think he was a little the worse for wear. Took the rest of the night off. I haven't seen him or that partner of his anywhere this morning."

"Nothing unusual about that. Professional gamblers don't usually get up and around until midafternoon.

"Meet any girls?" I asked, reaching for a juicy pear.

" 'Fraid not," he conceded, popping some raisins into his mouth. "But I had a right interesting night, anyway. When I got tired of watching poker, I went down on deck."

"Not a very smart thing to do, in the dark among that deck crew," I observed, realizing how much I sounded like a scolding father. "They seem to think every cabin passenger is loaded with money, and would welcome the chance to try to relieve him of some of it."

"Most of them were asleep, but I looked up Big John, just in case. Thought he was asleep, too, but he was prowling around somewhere on the starboard side near the stern. When I first got below, I heard some splashing back there. Guess he was heaving over an anchor or two to hold the stern from swinging into the bank.

"Anyway, I went stumbling around among all those

59

sleeping immigrants on deck. Woke up a few of them. All of a sudden Big John showed up with one or two Norwegians. The mate seemed startled to see a cabin passenger down on deck, until he struck a light and found out it was me. And then he got pretty mad."

"Why?"

"Don't know. Guess he was just out of sorts from lack of sleep, and everything that happened last night."

"What'd he say?" I took a big bite of the pear.

"Asked me what I wanted. When he found out all I wanted to do was talk and kill time, he ordered me topside. Said he was very busy. He left the definite impression that he was serious. And I wasn't about to argue."

"Strange. He seemed helpful and friendly enough through all that happened last night. Wonder how he could have been so busy. We were tied up for the night."

"Don't know. I'm not that familiar with a mate's duties. But even the engineer was asleep. Just one of his assistants on duty to watch the boiler gauges. But when Big John said, 'Git!' I got. But not before I noticed some commotion and stirring around among the deck passengers, up around the boiler area."

"Hell, if I had to sleep on a crate or a stack of cordwood or the hard deck, I'd be restless, too. Especially with all the mosquitoes that were probably working on them."

"Maybe so, but from what little I could see, it seemed more like somebody was sick."

"I'm still not surprised," I replied, refilling my coffee cup from the giant urn. "Those poor people probably have dysentery, worms, and every other ailment common to poor diet and exposure. I can still remember that packet ship my parents and I came from Ireland on—beating against westerlies for six weeks to cross the North Atlantic. Half of us poor, hungry Irish immigrants were sick all the way. Below deck, that ship stunk to high heavens. Quite a few of them died on the way. I remember at least four bodies being heaved over the side. And that captain would not even heave-to long enough for any kind of burial service." I shuddered at the long-forgotten memory.

"Most of our deck passengers are Irish and Scandinavian immigrants. Most of them are probably sick, too. You've never experienced it, Wiley, but poverty is a hard taskmaster."

Wiley seemed somewhat sobered by my remarks and didn't reply.

"We're all on this boat together, but we're kings compared to the squalor that exists down there. We are only separated by a few vertical feet, but we are in another world."

Wiley glanced around at the elegant appointments of the white-paneled saloon, at a group of gowned ladies walking past, and nodded his head in silent agreement.

My appetite was returning, and I grabbed a tart off the table and guided Wiley outside to catch the fresh breeze blowing off the river. We stopped on the broad forward end of the promenade deck, and I inhaled deeply of the morning air. It was a warm, bright June day, but the humidity of the previous day had been blown away, leaving the air invigorating. The green water spreading away from our wide bows looked cool and inviting. But I had done all the swimming in that river that I cared to do. From this height above the river, the force of the current and the twisting whirlpools did not look as formidable. The morning sun was sparkling off the water. As I squinted into the reflection I could just make out the shape of another boat coming into view from around a bend ahead of us. It was framed in my vision by the two landing stages that stuck up like giant horns at each side of our bow.

I moved to one side to get the glare out of my eyes and to watch the side-wheeler coming down the outside of the bend, its engines loafing, letting the current do the work, smoke drifting from the flared tops of its twin chimneys that towered at least seventy feet above the hurricane deck. It was a magnificent sight.

Our helmsman gave two short blasts of the steam whistle above our heads, and a few seconds later the other boat answered with two blasts to acknowledge that we would pass starboard to starboard. As the big, white boat drew closer, I could make out the name, *T. J. BYRNE,* painted in huge gold letters on her wheelhousing. Her main deck was jammed with cargo of all kinds—boxes, bales of cotton, barrels, cordwood for the furnaces, and even some cattle. As we slid by, passengers waved to each other from the decks.

As huge as this boat looked up close, she seemed the size of a toy compared to the immensity of the Mississippi. I watched her grow smaller and smaller and finally disappear around the next bend below us, leaving us alone on the river again.

"We should be coming up to Natchez before long, I suspect," Wiley commented, looking at the isolated sandbars and a thick stand of willows that stretched for a quarter-mile along the far bank.

"If Natchez-under-the-hill is as wild as I've heard, I'm staying aboard. I've had all the excitement I can stand for a couple of days," I answered, draining my coffee cup and savoring the isolation of the wilderness scene spread before me.

"I haven't been there in about eight years, but it was going hot and heavy then—gambling, drinking, knifings, and the like. But the old-timers tell me that place was in its heyday before you and I were born. I hear it was really something in the flatboat days before steam came along."

"Probably just an earlier version of some of the boom camps we've seen in the West." I rubbed a hand over the stubble on my jaw. "Think I'll go let the barber give me a shave. But before I do that, I'm going to get one of those hot baths. It's not often I have steam-heated running water. I need to soak the soreness out of my neck where I hit that water last night—besides getting some of this grime and river water off my hide." I turned to go back inside.

"Think we should look in on Staghorn?" Wiley asked.

"I hate to bother him if he's still sleeping; he needs the rest." I pulled out my watch. "But it's past nine-thirty. Maybe we ought to knock on his door, just to make sure he's okay."

We went through the saloon and knocked at the door marked "12." There was no reply. We knocked again and waited. Nothing. I tried the knob, but it was locked.

"Must've gone out somewhere."

"Yeah. Probably around the boat someplace. I'm going on back to get a bath and shave. How about setting my boots somewhere in the sun to dry?"

"Sure will."

"By the way," I said as we started for our rooms, "have you seen anything of the prince and his entourage this morning?"

"I saw three of his bodyguards at breakfast, but he must have eaten in his room or is still sleeping."

"Well, things should be quiet for a while, then. It

seems wherever he goes, there's trouble. I'll see you later."

Wiley started toward the outside, and as I walked toward my room, I noticed the wealthy planters, cotton merchants, what appeared to be various businessmen and several of their ladies taking advantage of the table of fruits and sweets. I wondered what those poor immigrants below were eating—or, for that matter, what they had eaten last night. None of them would be taking a bath in hot water this morning. Remembering my immigrant heritage and the poverty of my parents, I almost felt guilty at the luxury I was enjoying.

"There's the son-of-a-bitch that cost me a hundred bucks last night!"

I looked up sharply from turning the key in my stateroom door. For a second I didn't recognize the solidly built man in shirt-sleeves glaring at me.

"I think I'll take it out of your hide right now!"

I backed against the door and crouched as he moved toward me. But his companion, a nattily dressed man in a gray suit and derby hat, grabbed him by the arm. "Not now. It'll just get you in trouble. You should have done something about him last night."

"Hell, I tried to. If it hadn't been for that damn big mate, we'd have done it, too."

Then I recognized the broken-toothed sneer and the florid complexion of the man who had first attacked me for breaking up the fight. He dropped his clenched fists and I partially relaxed, taking a closer look at his calm companion in the gray suit. He looked vaguely familiar also. Then it dawned on me that he was the man at the edge of the crowd who was drawing a gun from under his coat when he was driven off by Prince Zarahoff.

"Who are you two, anyway?"

"Ron Whitlaw," the hatless one replied. "And don't you forget it. This here's my business partner, Mr. James Decker—just so's you'll know who you're payin' when you come up with five hundred dollars cash for the both of us."

"If you two want to bet on something, why don't you take up gambling with George Devol?" I countered. "I was just trying to keep a man from getting killed."

"Hell, I've tarred and feathered men for cheating at cockfights. You don't think I'm gonna let you take a hundred dollars out of my pocket like that and get away with it, do you? A sure bet canceled because of you? I'm not through with you yet. Before this trip's done, I'll have my money, with interest, from you or one of your buddies—and that includes that smart-ass foreigner you're tryin' to protect." Hatred burned in his eyes. He reluctantly allowed himself to be pulled away by the man in the gray suit who said something to him under his breath.

I let out the breath I was holding as I watched them go. My pounding heart let me know just how tense I was. Nothing like making new friends on a cruise, I reflected. Getting between a man and his money was almost as dangerous as questioning a lady's virtue. As old as I was, I should have learned that by now. But I probably would have done the same thing again, given the same set of circumstances. For all I knew, these two frustrated gamblers may have been the ones who threw the prince overboard or broke into his stateroom, trying to recoup their losses. In any case, I planned to be very wary of them from now on and be sure I went armed until I was safely off this boat. They didn't impress me as the types who would always fight with fists—especially the man in the suit.

***

I paid the barber and stepped out into the grand saloon, feeling clean, refreshed, rested, and ready for anything. It wasn't long in coming.

"We're steamin' up to Natchez," Wiley said, coming up. "I can't wait to get ashore and see if the place has changed any."

"We'll probably be there only long enough to take on or discharge some passengers and cargo. And I doubt if Natchez-under-the-hill really gets going until after dark. Besides, it's a little early in the day for a drink, even for you."

Just then, I looked up past Wiley to see the blond head and swollen eye of Fin Staghorn coming toward us. He looked worse than he had the night before.

"Morning. You look like you're still in a lot of pain," I greeted him, noting his grim expression. He didn't reply for a few seconds but came up to us and silently led us out of earshot of three men standing nearby. His face was even paler than I remembered it.

"Are you all right?" Wiley asked.

"I doubt if this boat stays long at Natchez," he said, slightly slurring his words around the still swollen lower lip, and ignoring Wiley's question.

"I imagine we'll be gone shortly after noon," I agreed, looking at him curiously.

"I just came from the main deck," he said, lowering his voice. "There is cholera aboard this boat!"

CHAPTER 7

"WHAAAT?" WILEY ASKED, AS IF HE COULDN'T TRUST his ears.

A chill went over me at the mention of this disease.

"Are you sure?" I asked, glancing around to see if anyone else was close enough to hear us.

"Absolutely. I've seen Asiatic cholera in the Far East."

Wiley and I looked at each other silently for a few seconds and then back at Staghorn, trying to absorb the shock of this news.

"That musta been what was goin' on down there last night when the mate ran me off," Wiley finally said.

"Who else knows about this?" I asked.

"I'm sure the crew knows. And all the deck passengers. I don't know about the cabin passengers. Most of them haven't been below. It stinks something awful down there. I saw three or four who don't look like they'll make it through the day."

"That wasn't an anchor they were heaving off the stern last night," Wiley continued, thinking out loud. "Big John and some of the crew were burying dead bodies."

"God! I can't think of anything worse, unless it would be bubonic plague."

A sudden, ominous cloud had darkened our luxury trip. I had seen a few cases of cholera myself, and it was not a pretty sight.

"There hasn't been a big outbreak of this in the Mississippi Valley since '73," Wiley said.

"Probably brought in on those immigrant ships at

New Orleans," Fin Staghorn guessed.

"Have you ever seen cholera?" I asked Wiley.

"No. Just read about it. I made sure I was out West last time it spread up this river."

"I saw cholera hit a man once, in Bombay," the sailor said. "He was walking down the street, feeling fine, then just doubled up and fell like someone had socked him in the stomach. He was dead inside of four hours. We put to sea as soon as we heard of the outbreak, but we lost four of our crew, and about six more were really sick."

"There's no cure?" Wiley asked.

"No. If you get it and survive, you're one of the few lucky ones. More than half the people who get it die, usually within a day."

"There are a lot of medical theories about what causes it," I said, "but nobody knows for sure. Thirty, forty years ago a lot of people thought it was the judgment of God for their sins."

"It's horrible to watch," Staghorn added. "Stomach and leg cramps, throwing up, a watery diarrhea they can't control."

"The body gets dehydrated in a short time. Can't keep anything on the stomach. Skin gets cool and dry, hands wrinkle, fingers start turning a bluish color. Usually go into a coma and die," I finished. I remembered these details from a newspaper story I'd written during the war.

"Well, what do we do now?" Wiley asked, looking at Staghorn and me, as if our previous experience with the disease somehow qualified us to do something about it.

"The crew's trying to keep it quiet to prevent a panic among the cabin passengers," Staghorn said. "But you can't keep a secret like that very long. There'll be a stampede to get off this boat as soon as she lands."

68

"As if those poor people on deck didn't have enough to suffer without this," I muttered as my first thrill of fear began to subside and I started to think of someone besides myself.

"I say we just sit tight and see what happens," Fin suggested. "Word's bound to leak out shortly. Crew's aware of it, so it's their problem now. Nothing we can do about it, anyway."

"I agree," I nodded.

Just then I sensed a change in the steady vibration of the engines through the carpeted deck under our feet. As one, we moved forward, out past the bar that was already doing a fair business. None of us spoke, our thoughts turning on the killer rampaging below. It was such a contrast to the sunny peace of the June morning that it was almost inconceivable.

A blast of the steam whistle signaled the townspeople of Natchez that we were nosing in toward the landing.

Hardly had the echo of the whistle died away than I saw a puff of white smoke and simultaneously heard a deep boom near the landing. An artillery shell whistled past our bow and, a few seconds later, exploded in a shower of mud and gravel on a sandbar on the far side of the river.

"Damn! They're shooting at us!"

Even from where I stood, I could hear a commotion and a jangle of bells in the pilothouse as the helmsman frantically signaled the engineer. The passengers were rushing out to the starboard side to find out what was going on. We were still a quarter-mile or so off the landing. Our paddle wheels gradually slowed to a stop.

"Ahoy, the *Silver Swan*!" a faint shout came from the shore. I shaded my eyes to pick out the man hailing us. The smoke from the fieldpiece was drifting upward on a slight breeze, and I caught sight of a gunner swabbing out the bore of the small, rifled cannon, just beyond the boat landing.

"Let's go topside and get a better view," Wiley said, and the three of us hurried up the nearby steps to the hurricane deck, It was already becoming crowded near the starboard rail.

"Ahoy, the *Silver Swan!*" came the cry again, this time louder. I still couldn't make out the speaker.

The short, red-faced, bewhiskered man who had broken up the confrontation between the prince and Devol the evening before pushed his way to the rail and raised a speaking trumpet to his mouth. "What the hell ya shootin' at us for?" he bellowed.

"Captain, we got word that you have cholera on board and . . ." A wave of excitement and a sudden babbling in the crowd around us drowned out the rest of his words.

"Shut up! Shut up so I can hear him!" the red-faced captain shouted. He raised the speaking trumpet again. "Why are you shooting at us?"

"Just a warning. You can't land here, Captain. We don't want the cholera. If you have passengers or cargo to land here, you can put in at Putnam's woodyard about two miles up. We're sending wagons up there to meet you. No one who has the disease can get off your vessel."

Muttering to himself, the bewhiskered captain pulled out a handkerchief and mopped his forehead and his balding pate. Without replying, he stomped away and climbed the steps to the pilothouse. I saw him talking to the helmsman and then heard the jangle of bells as the engineer was signaled. Through the big glass window I could see the pilot talking down the speaking tube to the

70

men somewhere on the lower deck who were laboring to keep the two big steam engines running. In a few seconds, both paddle wheels dug in and resumed their ponderous twenty revolutions per minute.

I don't even remember our charge upriver the two or three miles to the woodyard. The cabin passengers were in an uproar. Some of the men were white-faced with fear, others furious at not being told of the health menace. A few of the men and women were close to hysteria.

"Boy, he was ready to blow like a high-pressure boiler!" Wiley panted as we struggled through the milling crowd to reach the main saloon again. "You think he'll even bother to land at all?"

"He might just head to Vicksburg and hope to beat the news there."

"Not a chance," I offered. "They probably got a telegram from New Orleans when they discovered it there. The authorities probably guessed it was also infecting the immigrants going upriver and wired the towns along the way."

"Well, it's a damn shame," Wiley said, "but I guess these towns have been scourged by cholera quite a few times before, so I can't blame them for reacting the way they do."

"It's almost a way of life in some of the Far Eastern ports I've been to," Staghorn said.

It was only a few minutes before the big boat slowed once again and began easing in toward the starboard shore at the woodyard. Besides the woodhawks, we had a reception committee just as the man at Natchez had promised. A line of men with Winchesters stood along the high bank, grimly watching as the deckhands lowered our landing stages. A half-dozen empty wagons were pulled up a little farther back, their drivers calmly waiting, the teams stamping and swishing their tails at the biting flies.

Everyone was unusually quiet as Big John appeared on the main deck and began overseeing the roustabouts who were going ashore to get wood. Several of the cabin passengers also appeared below us on the main deck by the other gangway with their luggage, ready to disembark. A gray-haired man in a brown suit was examining each passenger stepping ashore.

Several roustabouts who weren't handling wood were busy rigging two forward booms for swinging some crates and whiskey barrels ashore. Our clerk stood to one side of the main deck, one foot propped on some cordwood, his pen and a receipt book balanced on his knee.

The loading and unloading went on amid an odd silence. The shock of their predicament seemed to settle in one those passengers who had just found out about the disease.

A sudden commotion behind us broke the ominous silence as we watched the scene below. Someone was demanding to see the captain. Before I even turned around I knew it was the voice of Prince Ferdinand Zarahoff, at its imperious best.

He stood near his stateroom door with his four retainers. He was dressed in one of his white, loose-fitting silk shirts, a pair of tight, whipcord breeches, and soft leather boots. From the look of his eyes, he had just been awakened, and from the sound of him, he didn't like the news he had just heard.

The captain was on shore near the end of a landing stage, talking to some official from Natchez.

"Bring the captain of this vessel to me at once!" the

prince demanded. "I am not going down below with that pestilence." He said something in Rumanian to one of his men, then took a pencil and a piece of paper and scribbled a note. One of his bodyguards, a tall, slim man with a prominent Adam's apple, took the note and quickly disappeared down the stairs. I saw him interrupt the captain, who tried to brush him off, but the tall man would not give up. I could not hear his words from where I was standing, but the rise and fall of the captain's voice told me all I needed to know. Finally, with the persistent gesturing of the prince's companion, the captain excused himself and followed the tall man back aboard and up to the grand saloon.

The captain would obviously rather have confronted the irate prince in a more private place, but that was not to be Prince Zarahoff hardly waited for him to get within earshot.

"Captain—Wilson, is it? Captain, I just learned of this cholera aboard. I have decided that my men and I will be going ashore here and now. We will go by rail the rest of the way to Saint Louis, and possibly on to Omaha."

He signaled over his shoulder to his men behind him. "Alex, start packing the gear. Quickly!" When they didn't respond immediately, he caught himself and apparently repeated the order in his native tongue.

"I'm sorry, Prince Zarahoff, but it won't be possible for you and your men to debark here," Captain Wilson said quietly. "The Natchez authorities will allow only those with tickets for Natchez to get off. And they have to be healthy. They don't want a flood of people descending on them who might bring the disease to their people. Surely you can understand that. They are taking a big enough chance allowing *anyone* to land."

"Captain Wilson," the prince said, obviously controlling his temper with a great effort, "my consort and I will be leaving this boat as soon as we are ready. I am a guest in your country, and I feel sure the officials of your government would be greatly displeased if they found out that you forcibly detained me and exposed me to a deadly disease. The relations between the United States and my father's regime in Rumania would be strained to the breaking point. Besides," he continued in a softer tone, as if explaining something to a dull child, "as you can see for yourself, we have not been directly exposed to the disease, and we are perfectly healthy." He turned away as if that ended the discussion.

Captain Wilson, obviously agitated, pulled out his handkerchief again and mopped his perspiring face. He looked around for some kind of support, but his officers and crew were apparently busy elsewhere. The cabin passengers who were within earshot had been temporarily distracted from their own fears and were watching attentively as this drama unfolded. No one made a move to interfere.

Finally, the red-faced captain decided he was on his own and would have to put up or shut up. In a quick movement, he reached inside his waistcoat and pulled out a nickel-plated Smith & Wesson and pointed it at Prince Zarahoff.

"This is for your own protection, Your Highness," the captain intoned, the incorrect royal title sounding strange in his mouth. "If I let you try to go ashore, those men down there with rifles will cut you down, royalty or no. They don't care who you are. They mean business."

The prince went livid and his eyes bulged. The heavy black mustache bristled as he started to reply, but he couldn't find the words.

Captain Wilson, seeing that he now had the edge, pressed his advantage. "I'm going to holster my gun. But all these people are my witnesses. If you and your men try to get off this boat and are shot, then it is completely your own fault. You have been warned." He slipped the big revolver back inside his coat and turned away, secure that he had won this round.

The prince was furious, as much at losing face as anything else, I guessed. But, during the exchange, I had seen him glance ashore at the line of men with Winchesters who stood grimly watching. Even though he blustered and swore under his breath at the captain as he went back into his stateroom and slammed the door, I think it was more for show than anything else. His reason was cooling his explosive temper. A man did not have to possess great intelligence to prefer taking his chances with cholera over defying the muzzles of those determined townsmen.

Captain Wilson climbed on a chair and shouted for quiet. He held up his arms. "Ladies and gentlemen, give me your attention. Please! Let me have your attention for just a moment." The buzzing of more than a hundred passengers gradually died.

"It's true that we have a few cases of cholera down below, but you are in no danger. Let me assure you of that." A hum of disbelief ran through the crowd. But Captain Wilson plunged on. "I've been on this river, boy and man, for thirty-five years, and in all that time, I've lived through five big outbreaks of cholera, and several smaller ones. I won't try to tell you it's not serious; you know better than that. But in all that time, I've seen only three cabin passengers die of it, at least on the boats I've been aboard of. As you can see, your chances of contracting this disease are very slim indeed.

If all of you will just remain calm, you have nothing to fear. We are doing all we can for the stricken deck passengers. We are obtaining a barge to tow behind us where we will separate all the infected from those still healthy. We will stop at some isolated spot at our earliest convenience and put everyone below ashore while we fumigate their quarters on the main deck. We plan to have everything under control before we reach Saint Louis. Even if we can't stop to take on provisions between here and there, we have plenty of stores. In fact, to make up for any inconvenience and uneasiness this may have caused you, I am instructing the bartenders to serve free drinks to any and all for the next two hours."

There was some grinning and nodding of heads at this. Sensing that he was winning over the hostile crowd, the captain continued, "I know that it is well past the dinner hour now, but the stewards will shortly be serving sandwiches and sliced cold turkey and ham. And the cooks will prepare a special meal this evening that will rival or surpass anything you have ever eaten." His voice rose with conviction as he warmed to his promises. "We will all feast together to show that this unfortunate occurrence will not get the best of us. We will come through unscathed. So drink up and enjoy yourselves!" He finished with a flourish, raising his arms to applause and cheers as the crowd broke up. Most of them made a rush for the bar at the forward end of the saloon. The white-jacketed stewards hurried to the kitchen to help the cooks.

"That was some performance," I remarked to Wiley and Staghorn as I reached in my pocket for my pipe.

"He knows how to win 'em over, all right," Wiley agreed. "Just open the bar. As soon as the crowd thins out a little, I think I'll take advantage of his generosity, too."

76

CHAPTER 8

IT WAS JUST OVER AN HOUR LATER THAT THE CARGO transfer was complete. The pilot gave a couple of short blasts on the whistle, the crew hoisted the landing stages, the lines were cast off, and we backed into midstream to continue our journey. But now there was a difference. We had an open barge in tow about twenty feet behind us. It was an unwieldy thing, about fifteen by thirty feet, two or three feet deep, and looked homemade. About a dozen of the sickest deck passengers were put into it on makeshift pallets, and furnished with buckets, some jugs of water, and towels. A few brave souls, apparently relatives, were there to take care of them. Those who were segregated in this barge were too sick to care, but now, instead of the heat of the boilers, they were exposed to the direct rays of the sun. And they were also exposed to the stares of the cabin passengers, many of whom were gathered on the hurricane deck, drinks in hand.

Captain Wilson and two or three of his officers circulated among the passengers trying to divert their attention by announcing that food was now available in the grand saloon. The crowd began to break up and drift in that direction.

"You'd think it was a travelin' circus!" Wiley snorted.

"I don't think so," I replied. "Look at their faces. They're looking down at all that agony and thinking that's what they're going to look like. Why do you think the crew is trying to get them away from watching this? When that sight sinks in and the liquor wears off, there'll be a stampede to get off at the next town. Not even the whole crew with guns will be able to stop them."

"You're right," Staghorn agreed. "I've seen panic before, and it's uglier and more dangerous than that cholera down there."

I glanced back at the scene below our stern. The Irish immigrants seemed to be the hardest hit. Some seemed comatose, some were retching into the buckets, and others sat, with only a blanket draping their shoulders, grimacing in the pain of diarrhea. I felt sure that many of them wore the only clothes they owned. My own stomach began twisting into a knot at the sight. I turned my back to the rail and took a long swallow of my beer.

"Maybe we oughta go down and try to help," Wiley suggested tentatively, after a long pause.

"Nobody—and that includes all these so-called doctors—knows what causes cholera, or how to cure it. The most we could do is try to comfort them, maybe try to get them to drink some water, even though they can't keep it down, maybe try to get them cleaned up." I shrugged with a nonchalance I didn't feel. "Some live; some die."

Wiley Jenkins wore a grieved expression, but he knew I was right and said nothing. He looked over the rail again, drained his glass, and set it on the deck. "Poor devils. Some o' them have already slipped into a coma that only the trumpet o' Gabriel will wake them from."

I started to remark that the Archangel Gabriel probably wouldn't be waking any devils, but thought better of it when I saw the serious look on Wiley's face. Finally, he came back and looked directly at me and Staghorn. In a very quiet, but intense, voice he said, "Don't you think we should *try*?"

78

In the silence that followed his question, I could hear the faint cries and groans over the noise of the machinery. My sympathy was with him and with those people of my former homeland, but the futility of it spoke to my head, rather than to my heart.

"The whole idea of going down below with that disease scares the hell out of me," the blond Staghorn said. "But you know what I do when something scares me."

I shrugged. "I guess I'll make it unanimous then. But if I keep listening to you two I'll have a hard time making it to my next birthday. Something's going to get me eventually anyway. This may not feel any worse than a bullet in the guts, Let's go."

"What do you three want?" a grim-faced John Wells greeted us almost as soon as we reached the main deck.

"We just came down to see if we could help." I tried to make my voice sincere and cheerful to mask the dread I actually felt.

"Nothin' you can do," he replied shortly. "Besides, if it should bust out on the cabin deck, you'll be blamed for spreadin' it."

"I've been in cholera outbreaks before in the Far East," Fin Staghorn told him, "and I can assure you that the danger of one person spreading it to another is almost nil."

Big John seemed to waver a bit. "Well, we could use a few extra hands. But I could lose my job for lettin' you down here."

"Don't worry about it. We'll take full responsibility. Just get busy and you'll never notice if we went back topside or not. You've done your duty and told us."

"Well, if you've got some experience with this disease, go to it." He waved us grandly past him.

"Frankly, it's got me buffaloed."

"You and a lot of medical people, too," I commented as we went on down the deck toward the heat of the furnaces. The moaning, retching victims were suddenly everywhere. Several Negro roustabouts were busy with mops and brooms swabbing and sweeping off the deck planks with buckets of river water.

"One of the best things they could do," Staghorn remarked. "Get all this filth cleaned up. All that vomit and watery diarrhea. If some of the sick have other clothes we should burn the ones they're wearing."

"We've already done that with some of them," a girl said. "If you want to do something, get a couple of those clean towels over there and help me." She was kneeling on the deck beside a pale, thin old man whose glassy stare indicated that he was far gone. As she looked up at us, I was struck by her beautiful, cameolike face, framed by short, black hair.

"Well, don't just stand there," she said, noting our slack expressions. "Get busy." She stood up—all five feet of her—and I saw that she was wearing a full-length white cotton apron over her summer frock. She had her sleeves pushed up above her elbows. Her brown eyes regarded us frankly. "If one of you gentlemen can stop gawking long enough, we could sure use some beef broth and some hot coffee. If we can get some nourishing liquids into these people, some of them may survive."

"Yes, ma'am," Wiley said, finally finding his voice. "That's the girl I saw at breakfast this morning," he said in an aside to me before he turned and dashed off toward the stairs to the cabin deck.

Fin and I got the towels. Using the clean water she had in a nearby bucket, we wiped the feverish brows of two of the victims. Then we began the nauseating task of cleaning up two more who were lying in their own vomit and excrement. Some of their clothes were mere rags and looked as if they were beyond salvage. We gave them to the firemen to throw into the furnace.

The relatives and friends of the afflicted ones were huddled around them, forming makeshift pillows for their heads, covering some with blankets in an attempt to keep them warm as their body temperatures dropped and their hands and nails took on a bluish cast. But for these victims, it was almost too late.

It was heartrending to hear their moans of pain. The soft murmurs of comfort or thanks, heavy with an Irish brogue, stirred deep feelings. I felt tears welling up in my eyes and had to turn my back and go to the railing, where I hung on a hogback brace until I could get my emotions under control. When I turned back, a woman broke into a wail, apparently just learning that someone had died. A younger woman put an arm around her shoulders and led her away. Most of the immigrants were not crying. Whatever their real feelings, they exhibited a numb acceptance of this latest calamity that had befallen them within a few days of reaching their new homes in this land of promise—a home free of the starvation and injustices of the old world. The Norwegian passengers seemed just as stoic. For people brought up on adversity, this was nothing more than expected.

"Mister!" The dark-haired girl was struggling to hold a big man as he retched violently into a bucket. "Help me!"

I jumped to her aid, my thoughts of pity vanishing in the urgency of the moment. The man she was struggling to hold weighed well over 200 pounds, but as each shuddering spasm passed, he was so weak he nearly fell forward into the bucket. When he finally stopped retching, we eased him back down on his side on a blanket. Staghorn was a few feet away, wiping the face of another man and helping him chew on a wet cloth to moisten his mouth.

Just then Wiley returned, swinging two one-gallon tin buckets with lids, and the two of us went from one to another of the victims, trying to nurse and coax a swallow of the broth or coffee down them. The problem was keeping it down.

". . . *sempiterna perducat.* Amen. *Benedicat te omnipotens Deus, Pater, et Filius, et Spiritus Sanctus.* Amen."

The Latin words sounded familiar. Near a stack of wooden cases a few feet away, a priest rose from his knees, a cloth stole still around his neck. He picked up his traveling case of holy oils and slipped it into his pocket. He was about six feet tall and lean, with sandy hair. His kindly face was set and serious.

"Father Fleming! Over here, please. It's my poor husband." The priest moved quickly to kneel beside an older man who looked up with a desperate but hopeful expression. The priest made the sign of the cross and began the last rites.

We spent the better part of the afternoon doing what little we could to comfort the sick and dying. It didn't take long for us to become totally forgetful of our own safety. Several times the barge was pulled in to our stern and new victims placed on it. The dead were brought back aboard, covered with old blankets or tattered canvas, and laid side by side on the after part of the deck.

About four o'clock Captain Wilson, true to his word, eased the big packet up alongside a towhead where we tied up. The towhead was thick with willows. Big John ordered everyone ashore from the main deck, the healthy helping or carrying the sick. I followed the dark-haired girl across the one gangway that had been lowered. Even though my mind was on other things, I couldn't help but notice the stunning figure moving under the light summer dress. When we were all ashore, the deckhands and a few of the Norwegian volunteers set about scrubbing down the decks and stanchions and rails from bow to stern. No sooner had they finished than smudge pots were lighted and placed on either side of the deck at the stern. The light breeze from the south blew billowing, foul-smelling smoke forward, smothering the entire deck. Even the engineer had to run for the stairs in order to breathe for a few minutes.

"Huh! Ridiculous waste of time!" the girl standing beside me exclaimed, addressing no one in particular.

"What is?" Wiley asked.

"Those smudge pots. That disease isn't in the air."

"How do you know?"

"They tried the same thing in New Orleans when we had an outbreak a few years ago. It didn't do anything but cause an awful, smelly fog in the whole city for several days. I didn't think we'd ever get that odor out of the curtains." She wrinkled her nose at the recollection. "The cholera just went right on and ran its course and, eventually died out as usual."

"What's your name?" Wiley asked, unable to contain his curiosity any longer.

"Ellen Vivrette," she replied, looking him directly in the eye. "And who are you?"

"Wiley Jenkins, ma'am."

She nodded, taking his outstretched hand briefly.

"You traveling alone?" he asked, offhandedly,

looking toward the *Silver Swan* that appeared to be afire from the thick smoke boiling from its lower deck.

"Only as far as Saint Louis. I'm going to visit a cousin there for a few weeks. Then I'm going on to Louisville to see an aunt and uncle."

"Were those relatives I saw you with this morning?"

"No. Just some friends of my family who've been in New Orleans on business. They're going back to Louisville. Or at least they were before all this happened."

As she spoke, I admired her soft, cultured accent, and noted her well-kept hands and nails and hair. Her clothes were not the most expensive, but were a long way from being the cheapest. She was obviously well educated and at least moderately well-off. She was also very self-assured.

There was a stirring of activity behind me, and I turned to see several men with shovels digging graves in the sandy dirt for the bodies that had been carried ashore. After several attempts, the gravediggers finally gave up trying to dig individual holes in the collapsing soil and just scooped out a long, shallow trench. All of the shrouded corpses were placed side by side in it.

We stood respectfully silent as Father Fleming read some short prayers for the dead, blessed the nine bodies, and then, closed the book. "God has a reason for everything," he said slowly to the crowd. "It was time for some of us to go to Him. Just as we are seeking a new earthly home in this new land of America, He has decided that their earthly work is done and has called them to their heavenly home. We should never be sad because they have been taken suddenly from us. Would you deny them a going home?"

With those words he turned and walked away. In the

few seconds that followed, the only sounds were the wind rustling softly through the willows, the swishing of the river's current past the towhead, and an explosive puffing of steam from the tall pipes aboard the boat. I was aware of some muffled sobbing and then the chinking of shovels as the mass grave was filled in.

Suddenly, I wanted this journey to be over. My nerves were stretched to the breaking point. The events of the past twenty-four hours had been just about more than I could take. I wanted to yell, or punch something—anything to relieve the tension and helpless frustration. Maybe a good, stiff drink and about twelve straight hours of peaceful oblivion in sleep would set me right.

Finally the smudge pots were put out and everyone was brought back aboard. We cast off and resumed our trip. Wiley, Fin, and I stayed below and tried to find the driest spots on the scrubbed deck to bed down the sick. More spare blankets were sent down by the captain as the sun dipped lower in the west and the air cooled slightly.

"If they just had decent food and the means to keep themselves clean," Ellen Vivrette lamented as we climbed the stairs to the main saloon and supper, "they would never have a problem with cholera."

"Ah, 'If wishes were horses . . .' " I replied.

"I know. I know. It's just so unfair," she said, obviously frustrated and tired like the rest of us. "Look at the luxury we're living in up here. Now what's fair about that, I ask you?"

I could think of no answer to her rhetorical question. In fact, the thought of her vanished entirely as we reached the promenade deck and the smell of delicious food reached my nostrils.

Captain Wilson had been true to his promise, and the cooks had outdone themselves. Wiley Jenkins, Staghorn, and I sat down to dinner forty-five minutes later after a bath and a change of clothes. I had never seen the variety and quantity of food that the white-coated waiters were setting on the snowy linen of the many tables. It was a meal truly fit for royalty, and I said as much to Wiley as I helped myself to a pile of mashed potatoes.

"Speaking of royalty, looks like Prince Zarahoff has decided to grace us with his presence this evening," Wiley said, inclining his head to his left. "Wonder why he's not eating up in the Texas at the captain's table, as usual?"

"He's probably still hot about that clash they had earlier today," Staghorn replied, spearing a thick slab of roast beef from the platter. His jaw was swollen, but it apparently wasn't going to affect his chewing. His eye was still discolored, but the swelling had subsided slightly so he could see out of a slit in the puffy flesh.

"That Ellen Vivrette is quite a woman," Staghorn remarked.

"I know," Wiley said. "I couldn't keep my eyes off her."

"I noticed."

"Do you think she's married?"

"I'd guess not from the way she talked. And I didn't see any rings on her hand."

"She had a lot of nerve going down there to help those people."

"I think she knows enough about the disease to believe she was in little danger of catching it," I added. "But it was still a courageous thing to do."

"Have you seen her since we sat down?"

"I think she's eating with those older friends of hers back aft toward the ladies' end of the cabin."

A crash of glassware interrupted us, and I almost choked on a half-swallowed piece of corn bread. A man at the second table from us had leapt to his feet, knocking over the wineglasses and his chair. He staggered back, holding his stomach and gagging. It was Prince Zarahoff! He doubled over and sank to his knees and then fell on his side, curled up on the carpet. The people at the nearby tables got to their feet and began crowding around as two of the prince's men rushed to his aid.

"What is it? What's wrong?" The crowd of diners buzzed louder with excitement as the clinking of silverware gradually ceased, and the piano player stopped.

"Is he sick, or choking?" a man cried.

"It's the sickness!"

"It's the cholera!"

I heard a scream that seemed to set off the panic, as people jumped to their feet and rushed to back away from the stricken man, knocking over chairs and spilling dishes.

"My God, I knew it would get us!" someone yelled over the confusion. "We're all doomed!"

CHAPTER 9

FIN STAGHORN NEVER HESITATED. THE WIRY SAILOR sprang forward and was kneeling beside the stricken prince almost before I realized what was happening. Fin was the only one trying to help; even the prince's four traveling companions were backing away.

Wiley and I got up and went over to see what we could do. Having worked around it all day, we had no fear of close contact with the disease. But it crossed my mind that someone might make the connection between us and the royal visitor rolling in agony on the floor. We had not been near the prince since about noon, before we went below, but most of the passengers didn't know that.

Staghorn bent low over Prince Zarahoff, who was curled up with stomach cramps and was weakly gagging.

Suddenly Fin jerked his head up, then leaned close to the prince's face again. "Has he just been eating something with garlic in it?" he asked sharply, glancing around at the people who were seated near the prince's party.

"Well, uh . . . no, leastways I don't think so," a tall, gangly man nearby replied slowly. "He'd not taken but a bite or two when he took sick."

Staghorn got to his feet and looked carefully at the prince's plate. Irish potatoes, yams, green beans, and a slab of roast beef. He sniffed cautiously at each, especially the roast beef. Then he grabbed a pewter pitcher of water from the table and sloshed some into a cup.

"Quick! Help me sit him up and get this water down him," he ordered me and Wiley over his shoulder. In a matter of seconds we had him propped up between us on the carpet and Fin was half forcing the water into his mouth. The prince coughed and choked a couple of times, but then began to drink. Fin tipped the cup up as fast as the sick man could swallow, spilling water down the silk shirtfront. He refilled the cup and went at it again.

"This man doesn't have cholera," he rasped quietly to us as he emptied the second cup and filled it again from the pitcher on the floor. "He's been poisoned."

"How do you know?" I asked, lowering my voice and glancing around.

"His breath smelled of garlic."

"So what?"

"His mashed potatoes have an odor of garlic, too, but the serving dish of potatoes on the table doesn't."

Wiley shook his head. "I still don't understand."

"Arsenic!" Fin whispered fiercely, forcing the prince's protesting mouth open for still another cup of water. "And plenty of water in a hurry is the only antidote I know for it."

We looked at each other but said nothing more. Staghorn continued to force water into the prince until he feebly protested he could hold no more. He still looked pale and shaky, but second by second he began to seem more alert. The violent retching stopped after he threw up the first two cupfuls of water.

"What's the problem now?" Captain Wilson asked, coming up with a worried look on his face to see what had disrupted his well-planned feast. "It's not the cholera, is it?" he asked, stooping and taking the prince by the shoulder.

"No," Staghorn replied. "This man has been poisoned. I think he'll be all right now," he hastened to add as he saw the look of alarm on the captain's face.

"There's nothing wrong with our food," the captain declared hotly but in a low voice.

"I don't know where it came from," Fin said, "but I am pretty sure it's arsenic. Do you have any of that aboard?"

"Well, yes . . . We have a problem now and again with rats in the hold."

"Do the cooks have access to it? Or is there any in the kitchen?"

"It's usually kept down below, but I guess they could get it if they wanted to. It's not locked up. My mate has charge of it. But I'm sure none of my crew would . . ."

He was interrupted by the violent, retching spasms of Prince Zarahoff as he vomited up more of the water and the viscous remains of his stomach's contents. Staghorn grabbed a linen napkin off the table, wiped the prince's mouth and mustache, and then began coaxing him to drink more water. "Come on," he urged, tilting the cup to the pallid lips, "we've got to dilute whatever is left of that poison." The prince nodded silently and did his best to swallow.

Who would want to poison Prince Zarahoff? Surely it was too coincidental to have been an accident. Until some answers were forthcoming, or until the prince was well enough to look after himself again, it seemed to me that somebody should be assigned to guard him day and night. I pulled the captain aside and said as much. He didn't answer immediately. He stood there, pulling at one bushy sideburn and staring thoughtfully at nothing.

"I can't really spare any of my crew for that kind of duty."

"Don't worry about that. One of us will do it until we get to Saint Louis."

"Why not let those four friends of his do it?"

"How do you know they're not the ones who tried to kill him?"

"For that matter, Tierney, how do I know you or your friends didn't do it?" he inquired, giving me a searching look.

"Do you think the sailor, there, would have come to his aid so fast? Hell, everyone else was backing off because they thought he had the cholera."

"Okay," he finally conceded. "I'll order him taken to my cabin up in the Texas. I have a spare bunk. Your blond friend there seems to know a good deal about medicine. Maybe he can look after him when I'm on duty. I'll leave word he's to have anything he needs for his care." He turned and gave the necessary orders to have the prince carried to his cabin. Immediately, two waiters, a cabin boy, and a clerk came forward and lifted the sagging man by his shoulders and legs. Staghorn walked in front, supporting the sick man's head, and the four Rumanians followed. The prince's face was a deathly pale, and he appeared to be going into shock.

"Damnedest trip I've been on lately," Captain Wilson muttered under his breath as he followed them out. "Maybe I need to retire."

"It's okay, everybody," he boomed as he went out. "The prince just has a touch of something. There's no cholera. There's no danger. Go on back to your dinner. He'll be all right."

Wiley and I went back to finish our meal, but not before I grabbed the prince's plate just as a steward was reaching for it. I brought it over and set it beside my own plate.

The hum of conversation resumed, along with the tinkling of silverware and dishes as the company settled back into their former routine. But my ravenous appetite was gone. Maybe it was the poisoned food on the table beside me. I forced a few bites down before I finally gave it up and took a long drink of water. I noticed Wiley, sitting across from me, having much the same problem.

"I don't need to be stuffing myself, anyway," he said with a weak smile as he saw me watching him.

"I know what you mean. I tell you what, why don't you dump this food of the prince's into a napkin and take it below. See if Big John can round you up a rat to test it on, so we'll be sure that's what it is. I'm going up and check on Staghorn and the prince. I'll meet you in the room in a bit."

"Right."

"We got some hot coffee laced with honey down him, and he's bedded down in the captain's cabin with plenty of blankets over him. He was getting a little color to his cheeks when I left," Staghorn said as he and I and Wiley sat in my cabin a little more than an hour later.

"You didn't leave him alone, did you?" I asked.

"No. Captain Wilson was there."

"What about those four cohorts of his?" Wiley wanted to know.

"Cap'n Wilson ran 'em off, on some pretext. They didn't like it, though. Don't know how long he'll be able to keep 'em at bay."

"Were you able to test that food?" I asked Wiley.

"Yeah. Big John hadn't emptied the rat traps lately. He got me a nice big one. I guess they don't have traps that kill 'em immediately so they don't rot and stink up the hold. Anyway, we put that food in a box with him

92

and he took right in after it."

"Well?" I urged as Wiley paused to sip a beer he had picked up on his way back to the room,

"Deader'n a hunk of stovewood inside one minute," he finished succinctly.

"Well, that settles that question," I said. "But how did you know it was arsenic, or how to treat it?" I inquired of Staghorn.

The young man leaned back in his chair and propped his feet on the bed.

"When you're months at sea without a doctor, you learn to diagnose and treat a lot of ailments, from food poisoning to broken bones to bad teeth," he began, rubbing his discolored cheekbone gingerly. "And I've been in a lot of rough ports, and seen a lot of the seamier side of life. Arsenic poisoning is just one of the experiences. Arsenic is usually a whitish powder. Whoever put it there knew it would blend well with the mashed potatoes. The prince apparently didn't have anything on his stomach, or the first couple of bites wouldn't have hit him so fast. That, and the fact that somebody sprinkled a pretty good dose on his potatoes when he wasn't looking. Arsenic has a distinctive garlicky smell. I might not have caught it except that none of the other food seemed to have any garlic in it, and there were no cloves or minced garlic on the table."

"Well, the obvious question is, who is trying to kill the prince and why?"

We looked at each other blankly.

"Seems we were asking this same question less than twenty-four hours ago."

We sat pondering this for a minute or two in silence. I reached for my pipe on the washstand and idly began packing it.

"I understand he's never been in this country before, so he couldn't have any enemies here," Staghorn said.

"Why not?" Wiley countered. "He's an arrogant foreigner who travels with servants and flashes a lot of money. How long do you think it takes to make enemies when you do that? There are some tough-looking characters on this boat who look like they would do in their own mothers for a dollar. And I'm not talking about deck passengers, either."

"You can't always tell about a person by the way he looks," I said.

"True. But did you see that crowd at the fight last night? They were positively bloodthirsty—even the women. Put that bunch in togas and they could have been in the Roman Colosseum watching the gladiators kill each other."

"But they were betting," I objected. "They weren't after the prince or his money."

"Still, I wouldn't put anything past some of those men, especially those guys who attacked us."

I thought of the two men who had threatened me this morning. "You're right." I went on to tell Wiley and Fin about the incident. "It may have been an idle threat," I finished, "but all three of us will have to be on our guard. Even if they are not the ones who are after the prince, they may be after us. If they can't get their gambling losses out of us one way, I'm convinced they'll try another."

"Well, if we're careful and stick together, we can protect ourselves. But that doesn't solve the prince's problem. Right now, he's in no position to protect himself. As I see it, our best chance to help him until he gets back on his feet and can fend for himself is to figure out who is trying to kill him," Wiley said.

"Maybe it's something political," I suggested, remembering the long turmoil between Ireland and England. "Maybe some attempt to assassinate him to create some trouble between our country and his."

"I haven't been keeping up on international events lately," Wiley remarked, "but I didn't know we've been having problems with Rumania. Hell, I'm not even sure where it is."

I shook my head. "Rumania got a monarch—something of a dictator, really—about twenty-five years ago, after a long, internal political struggle. That monarch is Prince Ferdinand Zarahoff's father. And that's about all I know about Rumania, aside from a few personal details of the prince's life that he told me the other night." I struck a match and applied it to my pipe bowl.

"You know, looking back on it," Wiley said, "I wonder if that fight with Devol wasn't a setup to get the prince beat up or killed. If we hadn't intervened, it would have probably turned out just that way." He shrugged and sipped his beer. "Maybe I'm just seeing goblins where they don't exist."

"It's possible, but we'll probably never know for sure. One thing we are sure of, though—somebody wants the prince dead. I presume it's the same person or persons who threw him and me overboard and put that arsenic in his food, figuring the symptoms would be mistaken for cholera."

"The question seems to be, what do we do about it now? Nothing? It's really none of our affair, although we've been drawn into it."

"I'm a live-and-let-live person," I said, puffing a cloud of smoke at the ceiling. "But when someone tries to kill me, it makes me damn mad. I don't necessarily

95

want revenge, but I'm all for cutting ourselves into the game on the prince's side, in case there's another attempt on his life. And I feel sure there will be. We could take turns staying with him day and night until he leaves the boat for good."

"I'm for that," Wiley said. "And I'm sure the prince will be, too. He's already asked Staghorn to be his personal bodyguard. What's wrong with a little part-time work until you get home, Fin? The prince would probably make it worth your while."

The sailor shifted his weight in the chair and ran his fingers through his shaggy hair. "I'm not interested in his money, but I'll do it. If a storm wants to take you one way, whether that's the way you're bound or not, you either have to heave-to, or run with it. And I never was one for heaving-to and drifting."

"How are we going to convince those buddies of his to let us stay with him?" Wiley asked.

We pondered this dilemma for a few moments.

"I think we just answered our own question," I said finally. "When the prince is well enough, get him to appoint Staghorn as his personal escort in this country. His cohort, or servants, or whoever they are, couldn't object if the prince, himself, orders it."

"But I might have to move across the saloon into their staterooms," Fin said.

"Tell the prince that one of us must accompany you, so that there will always be two of us to alternate when the other one is sleeping. Convince him that his four friends have not been successful so far in preventing attempts on his life. Maybe we can convince him to stay over here so we can keep an eye on him."

"That would probably work," he replied. "But if someone does succeed in killing him before he leaves the boat, there'll be hell to pay. We might even be accused, since we always seem to be around him."

"Well, it'll be up to us to make sure he stays alive and healthy."

"We'll either have to watch his food being prepared or have one of his friends sample everything before he eats it."

"You're right," I replied. "But I have a hunch that whoever is trying to do him in is smart enough to try some other method next time."

"You think there will be a next time, then?" Wiley asked.

"As sure as there's cholera on this boat. They may let the excitement die down and try it later. But if anyone is serious enough to throw him overboard and poison him, they're serious enough to keep trying until they succeed."

"Or get caught," Staghorn finished.

"If we even had some inkling why anyone would be trying to kill him, it might be easier to prevent another attempt."

"Whoever it is, he's trying to make it look like an accident."

"What about those four men traveling with him? Has anyone taken a good, close look at them?" Staghorn asked. We all looked at each other and shook our heads. I searched my memory, but couldn't even visualize the faces of the four, so much a part of the background had they been. "Has anyone heard them speak a word of English? Does anyone know their names or anything about them?" Again we looked vacantly at one another.

"That's a good place to start. We can get all that from the prince," Wiley said. "But we'd better be a little cautious about it. They may be related to him. They are, at least, trusted friends or servants, or they wouldn't be taking a trip with him. The prince might take offense if it sounds like we're questioning their integrity."

"We've got to start somewhere. If it's someone from this country who was out to get him, they'd probably just gun him down from ambush and let it go at that. Most Americans are not devious in their methods," Wiley said.

"With the possible exception of politicians and bankers," I added.

Conversation died and we sat with our own thoughts for a minute or two.

"Has Devol been around lately?" Wiley asked suddenly. In the excitement following the fight at the woodyard, I had forgotten all about the gambler.

"Nope. He's either been staying in his stateroom or he slipped ashore somewhere," Staghorn said.

"I would guess the latter. A man like that needs a well-ordered boat with well-heeled passengers to make a go of it."

"He's probably already hailed a boat going downriver by now, or is ensconced comfortably on some train, fleecing the passengers," Wiley said.

"Good riddance. We seem to have enough trouble without him." I was feeling very tired and irritable. "I wish I were off this boat and on my way to the Arizona Territory."

"Why don't you turn in?" Fin suggested. "After all, you older men need your rest." He gave me a mischievous grin. "I'll go up and see about the prince." He was up and going out the door before I could think of a suitable reply.

CHAPTER 10

I WONDER. WOULD THINGS HAVE TURNED OUT differently if cholera had been confined to the main deck or if the boat had been quarantined at the military post of Jefferson Barracks upon our arrival in Saint Louis? I really doubt it. What happened was probably inevitable. After the poisoning, Wiley, Fin, and I had all our attention on Prince Zarahoff and so were not attuned to what the rest of the cabin passengers were feeling. And apparently Captain Wilson was also blind to the general mood of his cabin passengers.

We had steamed slowly upriver, stopping only for wood. Even then we had to help ourselves and leave the money for the frightened woodhawks who had retreated to a safe distance when our boat nosed into shore. We had bypassed all river towns, including Vicksburg and Memphis, to reach Saint Louis the evening before. As Captain Wilson expected, we had been intercepted about five miles below the city by a small steam launch carrying a delegation from the city. The group included a doctor. We still had our barge in tow, but it was now empty. The disease had peaked and was apparently waning, with only a few new cases, and only one death in the past twenty-four hours. Things had begun to improve just after our burial detail on the towhead and a thorough cleansing of the boat. Captain Wilson had made it a point to provide food and water at no cost to the deck passengers. And, as a desperate preventive measure, he also supplied all the adult immigrants and deckhands with plenty of free liquor. But he was careful to limit the amount per person. Even so, several fights

99

had broken out among the crewmen, and one man had been knifed severely. Only five more deaths had occurred in the two days following the towhead burial, and they were the ones who were already far gone with cholera. Their bodies were weighted and sunk in the river.

The Saint Louis doctor in the boarding party who inspected the *Silver Swan* had wanted to quarantine our boat at Jefferson Barracks, just below the city, as was the normal procedure. But, at the captain's pleading, the doctor had finally allowed us to tie up at the city boat landing. He posted yellow quarantine signs on the boat and forbade anyone to go ashore except those half-dozen acutely ill passengers and two crewmen who were taken to a marine hospital.

I don't believe the reaction that followed would have happened if two cabin passengers hadn't suddenly fallen sick late in the evening of our arrival. The crew tried to keep it quiet, but word spread like a blaze of heat lightning that the unseen killer had finally invaded the first-class compartments and was silently stalking its inhabitants. After supper, the main saloon was abuzz with rumors and speculation, bordering on outright panic. Men and women stood about nervously in small groups, talking quietly and glancing often at the closed stateroom doors where the two victims, an elderly man and a twelve-year-old girl, were lying sick. They were being attended by their families and assisted by Ellen Vivrette, the clerk and the second mate. Almost none of the passengers went about the usual after-dinner pursuits of walking on the decks, crowding the bar, or playing cribbage or poker. Even George Devol, who had surfaced after a day or so of staying out of sight, had no luck in luring his usual number of customers into a game. Interest in his type of gambling had fallen off sharply after the flare-up with the prince and his fight with Staghorn. Instead of deserting the boat as we had suspected, he had only remained in his room for a day or so, resting and allowing his bruises to heal. Since resuming his gaming activities, he had a few regular, well-heeled customers who patronized his table every evening, but they seemed to win about as much as they lost, which led me to suspect that they were plants.

This first evening of our arrival in Saint Louis, Devol made several desultory attempts at three-card monte, but his first two customers lost a few dollars and drifted away from the table to join the groups of fearful passengers.

"Come, come, ladies and gentlemen," Devol called, riffling a pack of cards in his big hands, "how about a game to while away the time? What's your pleasure— monte? faro? blackjack? Chose your game and maybe Lady Luck will fatten your poke tonight."

Wiley, Staghorn, and I were lounging at the bar and could hear his persuasive voice clearly from about forty feet away. From the reaction he was getting from the passengers, he might not have even been there. Finally, after one or two more attempts at drumming up business, he put his cards away, folded up his board, and prepared to call it a night. Even a man like Devol, who did more suckering than gambling, couldn't make a profit if he couldn't lure customers. Besides, I'm sure he sensed the ominous tension in the air.

What followed next is difficult to sort out in my memory. Darkness had just fallen when word came that the elderly man had died, only a few hours after contracting cholera. I could almost see the news rolling across the long room toward me, like wind across a wheat field. Then a woman screamed and that set off the panic. There was a simultaneous shuffling of many feet on the carpeted deck as the crowd shifted toward the forward end of the boat and the stairway. Then the movement broke into a rush and the stampede was on. I could hardly believe what I was seeing.

"Outa my way! I'm gettin' off this boat!" someone yelled. A body slammed into me, and my glass of beer went crashing to the deck. I grabbed for the bar as I was spun around. Wiley had hold of my arm to keep me from being swept out the door with the tide of wild-eyed passengers. The deck quivered under the thunder of running feet. I faintly heard the splintering of wood as the bannister gave way, followed by shrill cries of pain.

"C'mon! This way!" I was vaguely aware of someone shouting in my ear. Then Staghorn was pulling me along the edge of the bar back into the big saloon. Not everyone had run for the stairs. About twenty people were scattering toward their staterooms. As we dodged around the litter of overturned chairs and tables, I caught sight of George Devol, calmly leaning against a table, his arms folded across his chest. The look on his face was one of amused tolerance as he watched more than a hundred bodies jamming the forward stairway. Human nature was an open book to this man.

We reached Fin's room, and it took him only a few seconds to find the key and unlock the door. We bounded across the room, and as we burst through the opposite door to the outside promenade deck, we were almost run down by two burly men trundling a heavy trunk between them. Several more men and women shouldered past us, eyes fixed ahead and unseeing. As they neared the forward end of the big boat, they began wildly pitching their luggage over the rail. But these few who had gone back for their belongings should have taken a little more time and carried their luggage below. Bundles rolled in blankets, carpetbags, handbags, and leather grips went spinning over the side, some to crash on the lower deck, some to bounce on the guard rails and into the edge of the river. Only a few of the lighter, better-aimed bags landed safely on the cobblestones.

I grabbed a stanchion and leaned out over the railing. The main deck was chaos. The cabin passengers were rushing wildly to get ashore. No landing stage had been lowered, but the panicky passengers were climbing the guards and dropping the few feet to the landing. As I looked, one woman caught her long skirt and tore it half off as she fell into the edge of the water about five feet below. A man tried to protect his wife from the surging crowd, but panic knows no chivalry. Women were shoved aside, knocked down, and trampled in the rush. Everyone was shouting and screaming in rage or fear or pain as the crew began a late rally in a vain attempt to stem this surprise onslaught. It was full dark. The only faint light illuminating the struggling mass of humanity came from the few distant gas lights and a row of lighted windows and doors on the packet moored just to our port side.

"Dammit, get back up there, you bunch of cowards!" It was the voice of Big John Wells, the mate. His giant form loomed up out of the shadows on my side of the boat. With one sweep of a mighty arm, he hooked a man away from the guard and hurled him back into three others. Directly below me I could faintly make out some of the immigrant deck passengers trying to huddle back out of the way of the well-dressed crazy people who were invading their deck of the *Silver Swan*.

"Hold 'em back from that side!" Wells shouted at a

deckhand, giving him a shove forward. But the deckhands were too slow and too few to do much good. They were overwhelmed by the mass of bodies swarming like ants and dropping safely over the side.

Just then I was astonished to see the lavender silk shirt of Prince Zarahoff catch the faint light as he appeared near Big John. He threw a punch at a nearby man whose bulk was crushing an older woman against the rail. The forms were indistinct, but it appeared that the prince's four bodyguards had struggled to his side and were aiding him in his effort to halt the quarantined passengers.

"Go back! Go back! You are safe!" I heard him shout in his distinctive accent. "There is more disease on this lower deck than in your own quarters. Go back! The authorities . . ."

I was so engrossed in this scene that I wasn't aware of Staghorn climbing over the rail and down a stanchion to the lower deck. Quick and agile as a cat, the seaman was into the seething mass below before I could grab him. Instead of trying to prevent the escape of the passengers, his concern was to protect the women who had been knocked down and were being crushed in the mob.

Somewhere in the distance I heard a whistle as the watchman who had been assigned to guard the quarantined boat spread the alarm. Dark figures ran and limped up the landing, scattering away from the boat in all directions. A police paddy wagon, drawn by a team of horses, came clattering into view under the gaslights, followed quickly by another.

Saint Louis police fired several shots into the air and quickly had the situation in hand. The remaining passengers were herded back to the cabin deck, looking disheveled and scared, as if they were being forced back into their death chamber. Instead of returning to their staterooms, most of them huddled like frightened sheep in the middle of the grand saloon until an ambulance arrived about twenty minutes later, bearing a doctor and two attendants. They took away the covered body of the elderly cholera victim. Then they herded the little girl and her parents ashore and into the ambulance.

Following some hollow-sounding assurances by Captain Wilson that there was no more danger of infection, most of the remaining passengers reluctantly retired to their staterooms, while a few of them repaired to the bar to bolster their courage and kill any lingering germs in their systems.

George Devol still sat alone at a table in the saloon, a gold toothpick in the corner of his mouth, watching the passing parade. Either he had no fear of cholera, or else he had been held in place by that peculiar fatalism that all professional gamblers seem to have.

"Think they'll ever catch the ones who got ashore?" I asked as Wiley, Fin, and I gathered at the bar.

"I doubt it. They may round up a few, but I'm sure some of them will never be back. They'd face anything, including jail, before they'd come back to this boat and face what most of them see as certain death," Staghorn said. "People usually fear what they can't see or understand."

"Anybody get hurt in that melee?"

"I saw the purser bandaging up some heads a few minutes ago," Wiley replied.

"There were some cuts and bruises, and I think a woman may have broken her ankle," Staghorn added.

"I can't believe the prince and his men were down there, trying to help."

"Surprised me too," Fin commented. "Especially since he was the one who nearly shot his way off the boat a few days ago at Natchez."

"Yeah. Seems like he would have run with the rest of 'em," Wiley Jenkins said.

"He might demand his rights and stalk off the boat with his servants carrying his luggage, but he's not the type to run scared with a bunch of panic-stricken passengers. That's not his style," I said.

"I don't think any of us really knows what his style is," Fin reflected. "Just when we think we have him pegged, he does something that surprises us. He's his own man, I guess, or else just contrary as hell."

"Maybe he figures to jump ship himself, and knew security would be tightened if we didn't quell this riot ourselves before it got out of hand," I suggested.

Things seemed to be settling down for the night. There was a police patrol on guard on the landing to ensure against any further attempts at escape. We decided to finish our drinks and retire to our staterooms.

"Hey, kid!" George Devol called as we passed him in the saloon.

Staghorn paused, a look of irritation on his battered face.

"My name is Fin Staghorn."

"Whatever. You and your friends have caused me considerable grief and pain. It might have been worth it, except that while you were slugging me with that sneak punch here on the boat, someone got away with the stack of gold coins I had just won from your Rumanian friend. I'm not a man who works for nothing. I intend to recover that gold."

"What makes you think we've got it?" Fin asked. "It could have been anyone standing around that table.

106

There was quite a crowd."

"It doesn't matter. If you hadn't distracted my attention, the money would not have been stolen. Tell your friend I'll be around to see him. He knows how much it was. Between the two of you, you had better come up with it."

"Or?"

"I'll have the great satisfaction of taking it out of his royal hide—and maybe yours, too."

"Would attempted murder be one of your alternatives?" I asked as we moved away. The poker face behind the graying goatee gave no hint that he knew what I was talking about.

CHAPTER 11

"Yankee ship come down the river,
Blow, boys, blow!
Her masts and yards, they shone like silver,
Blow, my bully boys, blow!

"Have you ever been to the Congo River?
Blow, boys, blow!
Her fever makes the white man shiver,
Blow, my bully boys, blow!"

"YOU'RE FEELING MIGHTY GOOD THIS MORNING," I remarked, stepping out onto the promenade deck. "But I'd almost prefer that Congo River fever to what we've been through this past week."

Fin Staghorn abruptly stopped singing the chantey and turned to face me with a grin. "Beautiful morning, isn't it?" He swept his hand at the Saint Louis skyline

107

spread before us, sweltering in the heat of the midsummer sun.

"Where's the prince?" I asked.

Staghorn inclined his head, and I followed his glance to see Prince Ferdinand sitting in one of the wooden deck chairs nearby. He was still looking a bit subdued, but his health had fully returned.

I smiled at Staghorn as I leaned on the rail with my cup of coffee. "I think we ought to congratulate ourselves on protecting him since that poisoning attempt. Nobody's bothered him since, not even in that panic the night we arrived. Someone could have put out his lights for good in that mob and made it look accidental."

"We're not out of the woods yet," Fin replied, lowering his voice slightly as he glanced up the deck toward the prince, who was dozing in his chair. "Whoever tried to kill him is just lying low until they get another good opportunity. I doubt if we'll see anybody try anything when we're watching him day and night."

"Any trouble from Devol or that other character . . . Whitlaw?"

"No. They may be waiting their chance, or else they were both just mad and making idle threats."

"I don't know. I wouldn't ever underestimate the enemy."

"We'll just have to keep eyes in all sides of our heads, even when we're asleep."

"Wonder how long they'll keep us quarantined?"

Staghorn shrugged, running a hand through his shaggy blond hair. "Hope it's not long. I can think of places I'd rather be than here." He stared out over the haze of smoke and heat rising from the jumble of buildings that were jammed together for miles in each direction. Our boat was nosed in at an angle to the landing between two other large packets. The cobblestone landing sloped up from the water about 150 yards to end at a row of drab brick warehouses and smoke-blackened buildings that lined the waterfront.

"About the only good thing I can say about this enforced confinement is that it gives me time to get to know Ellen Vivrette. She's quite a woman. Got a mind of her own."

"Not to mention a body. Wiley seems pretty taken with her, too."

"Yeah." Fin grinned and unconsciously put his hand to his left cheekbone, which was still discolored. However, the swelling was gone and his eye was undamaged. "And he's got it over me in the looks department. I guess, to be right truthful about it, he's been visiting and eating with her and out walking the hurricane deck in the moonlight a lot more than I have."

I pitched the dregs of my coffee over the rail, then slipped my watch out and popped it open. "Wonder how long till lunch?"

"Hell, it's only been about an hour since breakfast."

"I know. Guess I'm getting bored. Wiley's still in bed. He was up most of the night keeping an eye on the prince. Don't know how he sleeps during the day in this heat."

"I'll be breathing a lot easier when we turn the prince over to Buffalo Bill. I don't know why I ever took on this job. I'm a sailor, not a bodyguard."

"What boat are we going upriver on?"

"I'm not sure. One of those Benton Line mountain packets."

"Hope they'll take us aboard. Everybody seems

scared to death of this cholera."

"They'd better take me aboard, or I'll let 'em hear about it."

"Where does the prince meet Buffalo Bill?"

"Not real sure, and I didn't ask him. I believe I did hear him mention something about Bismarck, though."

"You know, I have a strange feeling about those four characters traveling with him."

"I do too." Fin nodded. "But I can't put my finger on the reason why. Maybe it's just that they don't speak a word of English."

"Have you ever heard them say anything? You two have been taking most of the guard duty."

"They talk to each other some. I didn't recognize the language, but I guess it must be Rumanian. And Wiley and I did get their names—Karl, Nicolae, Ion, and Alex. Putting the name to the face is about all we've done."

"Do any of them strike you as sneaky or sly or vicious? Anything out of the ordinary? I still have a feeling they're mixed up in these attempts on the prince's life."

Staghorn pondered the question before he answered. "Pretty hard to tell. None of them has made any suspicious moves. But then, we didn't expect them to while we were right there. The one named Alex is all muscle. He's short, but I'll bet he could bend an iron bar with his bare hands. Ion is the tall, skinny one with the big Adam's apple, and the eyes like a sad hound. Very neat and fussy about his personal appearance. He seems harmless enough. Karl is the one with the full beard who's about your size. He seems to be the quietest. Nicolae is the biggest of the four. He probably weighs around two thirty, and it's more muscle than fat. He strikes me as a scheming one, but that's just a hunch; I

110

have no way of knowing for sure. One thing about him, though. He has some kind of skin condition on his hands. They look scaly, like there's dead skin flaking off them all the time. They look rough and callused, like he's been doing constant manual labor."

"Hmmm. You didn't ask Prince Zarahoff about them, did you?"

"I brought up the subject. Turns out he doesn't know those men very well. They are members of some sort of elite palace guard. His father appointed them to look after him on this trip. The king apparently has a lot of enemies and he wanted to be sure nothing happened to his son in America. The prince didn't say so in so many words, but I get the distinct feeling that he wishes they hadn't come at all."

Something he had just said struck a familiar chord in the back of my mind, but it slipped away before I could grasp what it was. I tried to focus on it, but it was gone.

Just then Prince Ferdinand Zarahoff got up and came toward us.

"Ah, gentlemen, it appears we're to be marooned here for a time." Perspiration was beaded on the olive skin of his forehead.

"Looks that way," Staghorn answered, eyeing him critically.

The prince wiped a hand across his face. "I'm regaining my strength rapidly, but I wish it were not quite so hot. The summers in my country are not quite so . . . moist." The poisoning seemed to have taken some of the haughtiness out of him. He was friendlier than before.

"Would you gentlemen care to join me at the refreshment table inside? No? Then you will please we excuse me for now." He nodded and walked away and disappeared around the forward end of the deck.

"Let's go up here so I can at least keep an eye on him through the doorway," Fin said. "He may not like to feel someone is playing nursemaid to him, but I don't want to let him out of our sight for a minute."

"Fin!" I stopped suddenly and grabbed his arm.

"What?" He looked startled.

"I just remembered something. You said one of the prince's men had rough, scaly hands."

"Nicolae."

"Right. Well, it just dawned on me that some of the hands that slung me over the side that night were very rough. I was pretty groggy, but I remember them swinging me back and forth before they tossed me. Felt like my wrists were being sanded."

Staghorn stopped and looked at me thoughtfully. "Well, it's not positive proof, but it's a good start. Do you remember anything else? How many men were there?"

"Only two. Or at least there were two who pushed the prince over. When I came around the Texas after them, I don't know how many there were. I never saw them. Then when they hit me I was so stunned, I couldn't tell. But whoever it was seemed incredibly strong."

"Maybe that muscle-bound Alex and the rough-handed Nicolae."

"Maybe."

"Did they say anything?"

I stretched my powers of recall back to that night of pain and fear. "I don't know . . . they said something to each other, but I don't remember . . . I was hurting so bad. That punch in the belly damn near paralyzed my diaphragm. Lucky they didn't hit me in the ribs."

"Do you remember anything they said? Even one word?"

I struggled with the painful memory again. "It's no use. I can't remember. I guess I was so shocked, I wasn't really aware of what was going on. No, I don't recall a word."

"Could they have been speaking something besides English? Maybe Rumanian?"

"It's possible, but I can't be sure. There are other people on this boat who don't speak English. Those Norwegians on the main deck, for example."

"You're right."

We resumed walking.

"Do you think we ought to tell the prince about this?" I asked.

"Why not? Those men were appointed by his father, and he may be suspicious about them. At least they aren't close friends or relatives of his."

"If we can just stay between the prince and those four until we meet Buffalo Bill and his party, then our responsibility is ended. We'll just tell the scout what we suspect and let him take it from there. Besides, the prince is a grown man. He should be able to take care of himself."

Staghorn looked sideways at me. "We both know better than that. If someone was determined to kill you, do you think you could prevent it without a little help? Especially if you didn't know who it was? Besides, I have a feeling there'll be a lot more developments before we get to Bismarck. I think we ought to take it a day at a time."

We came out from under the overhead shade, and the sun bore down on us with all its force. We faced around, looking in vain for a breeze. I was wearing no hat, and the sun felt as if it were shining through a magnifying glass onto the top of my head.

"Whew, let's get inside out of this," Fin said. "I could use a cold beer."

We stepped into the grand saloon and up to the bar. We could sip our beer and watch Prince Zarahoff. He was standing by the table of food, munching some raisins and conversing with a few of the passengers. As we looked, all four of his men came out of their suite of rooms and walked over to the table near him. I looked at them with renewed interest. Were those the hands of potential killers? At least now I would have some idea about where to look and what to be careful of. I certainly hoped I wasn't looking in the wrong direction.

The sweltering day dragged on, with us still guarding the young prince, two men on and one off. A light lunch was served, and Wiley Jenkins and I took over our apparently casual observance of the prince while Staghorn took a nap. The royal visitor also retired to his stateroom after lunch, leaving both doors propped open to catch any semblance of a breeze that might be lurking around the waterfront. I took a chair just outside his door on the deck while Wiley stationed himself, drink in hand, inside the main saloon. Alex, Ion, Karl, and Nicolae entertained themselves by playing cards at a table in the saloon. I thought it rather odd that they were not offended by our intrusion on their domain as companions to the prince. To me, Wiley, and Fin, there appeared only two explanations for this attitude: Either they were hired hands who were glad to be relieved of their responsibility, or they were the ones trying to kill him, and were biding their time, waiting for another opportunity to make it look like an accident.

It was midafternoon before Fin and I got the opportunity to catch the prince alone and tell him of our suspicions. Even as I spoke, my reasons that had seemed so logical earlier now sounded vague. He heard us out before speaking.

"I appreciate your concern, gentlemen," he replied. "And I will take your warnings seriously. But I don't really feel that these men should be accused until we know for sure. I have considered the possibility also, but I have dismissed it as most unlikely."

"Why?"

"First of all, these four men were members of my father's palace guard. The men who form this guard are carefully screened. They have performed well in the army and have proven their dedication to our country. It is a very high honor to be selected for the palace guard. They number only fifty men.

"Secondly, we made a voyage of several weeks together, and no attempt was made on my life until we reached this country and this boat. Had these four men been my enemies, they would have had ample opportunity to arrange for my demise on the high seas. We encountered two storms of several days each in our passage. There were many times when I could have conveniently vanished overboard.

"Then, during the few days we spent in New Orleans, I read of several murders. Certain parts of that city are apparently notorious for robbery and murder. And yet, no attempt was made on my life there. No, gentlemen, I'm afraid you are wrong. No attempts were made on my life until we boarded this elegant boat. As much as I would like to find out who is behind all this, I'm afraid my companions are not involved." He shrugged. "It could be that the rougher element among your countrymen resent my presence. Wealth, breeding, and power seem to inflame the passions of some men, especially those who are not accustomed to seeing it."

I could see Fin's face reddening as he sensed a slur against Americans. He started to retort but choked back his words. "But what do you really know about these men?" he finally managed to ask. "Couldn't they be ambitious for your money or your power?"

"Hardly. By killing me they would not ascend to power in my country. And as for money, they are reasonably well paid. Their recompense is more than double that of the average soldier, and their quarters at the palace are nearly as luxurious as our accommodations on this boat. So what possible motive could they have?" He looked from one to the other of us and nodded curdy, indicating an end of the discussion.

The rest of the day and the night passed uneventfully, and the next day seemed almost a duplicate. No word came from the health authorities of Saint Louis about how long our enforced detainment might continue. The boat's crew and die cabin passengers were restless but seemed to understand the need for the quarantine and took it in stride. Captain Wilson was the exception. He paced the boat like a caged lion, back and forth through the grand saloon, up to the hurricane deck, up into the pilothouse and back through again. About every other round trip, he picked up a drink from the bar and, thus fortified against contagion, went below to tour the main deck. As the day wore on and became hotter and stickier, he shed his coat, his top hat, his tie, and wound up each day with his sleeves rolled up to the elbows, his shirt soaked with sweat, red-faced, disheveled, and more than a little drunk.

We were even denied the company of the pretty Ellen Vivrette, who spent most of both days below on the main deck, succoring those who were still sick. We had had no deaths in more than forty-eight hours, and those still under the influence of cholera seemed to be slowly recovering. A doctor spent two or three hours aboard each day, administering calomel and opium at the first symptoms, directing the disinfecting of the lower deck, and ordering the personal hygiene of the deck passengers.

"Do you think they might turn us loose tomorrow?" Wiley wondered aloud as we sat around the table in the main saloon after dinner on the fourth night in port. "From the looks of this dinner, we're about to give outa grub."

"Not much chance until everyone below is healthy, and the authorities feel sure there is no danger of spreading the disease to the city," I replied, propping my feet up on the chair opposite me and packing my pipe. "But you can do without food as long as the bar doesn't run dry."

He grinned at me. "You're right. What am I getting all nervous about? Might as well enjoy the luxury of this floating hotel as long as I can. Which reminds me, I've been on guard all afternoon. Think I'll go get a good bath, have a beer, and turn in. I'm tired." He glanced around as he got up. "You haven't seen Ellen . . . er, Miss Vivrette around here during supper, have you?"

"Nope," Fin replied smugly. "She must be taking her meals in her cabin. Haven't seen her in here all day."

It was nearly nine o'clock. Dinner was being served later to take advantage of the slightly cooler hours of darkness.

"I guess it's the two of us who bed down in the prince's stateroom tonight," I said to Staghorn after

Wiley had gone. "I don't relish bunking on the floor when there are good beds on this boat."

"Why don't you take the other bed in the prince's room?" Fin said. "I'll take the floor."

"No. It's my turn."

He pondered this for a moment. "Then why not do this—you sleep in your own stateroom and let me guard the prince alone."

"Too dangerous. We agreed to guard him two at a time."

"I'll lock the door to the adjoining room where his four friends sleep. Besides"—he hurried on when he saw I was going to object—"I'll have your Colt under my pillow, and I'm a light sleeper. Comes of standing watches at sea for six years."

I was sorely tempted, but I didn't want to give in to my craving for a soft bed. Especially in front of someone who thought a man of thirty-four was middle-aged.

"Oh, go ahead," he urged. "Nothing has happened so far, and nothing will happen tonight. Give me your gun."

When I still hesitated, he insisted. "Give me your gun."

I slipped it out of my holster, checked it to be sure there were five loads in the cylinders with the hammer resting on an empty chamber, and handed it to him.

"Thanks. Now if you'll excuse me, I have to go to the head before I turn in. The prince wants to go to bed early tonight. He's still building up his strength. See you in the morning."

I don't know how long I had been asleep when I was jarred awake by someone shaking my shoulder. For a second or two I thought it was morning and Wiley was

118

waking me. But when I opened my eyes to blackness, I jerked awake quickly.

"Shh! Be quiet. It's me—Fin."

"What's wrong? What time is it?" I answered in a hoarse whisper.

"The prince. He's gone."

"Gone?"

"Slipped out somehow after I was asleep. I can't find him anywhere, not even on the main deck. I think he must have gone ashore."

I was already sitting up and dressing as he spoke. We didn't strike a light for fear of waking Wiley in the adjoining room.

"But the worst of it," Fin continued, "is that two of his men are gone, too—Alex and Nicolae."

CHAPTER 12

I FINISHED DRESSING IN THE DARK AND THEN GUIDED Fin quietly through the door to the outside deck.

"How long have they been gone?"

"Don't know for sure. It's about half past twelve now. I guess less than an hour and a half. I must have dozed off in the chair about eleven. And the last I remember, the prince was sitting up, reading. The other four had gone into their adjoining stateroom, and I'd locked that door. So I don't know if they were still there or not."

I paused near the forward end of the promenade deck and tried to organize my thoughts. The only coolness provided by the still night air was a feeling of dampness coming off the river.

"You say you've searched the boat and they're not aboard?"

"Not unless they're hiding somewhere."

"Does the prince have any lady friends aboard?"

"None that I know of, even though three or four have been trying to weasel into his company this week. Impressed by his title mostly."

"Hmmm." Where could they be? My mind was in a whirl. It might be nothing, but then again, if our suspicions were correct, the prince's life might be in deadly danger. He could already be dead. It was too much of a coincidence that his two retainers had turned up missing at the same time.

"Did you ask those other two?"

"Yeah. All I got was a shrug. They can't speak English, and I don't know if they're just playing dumb about understanding it. I know they got my meaning, but they couldn't, or wouldn't, tell me anything."

"They must have somehow slipped ashore," I finally said, concluding aloud my train of thought.

"I think so," Fin agreed. "But why didn't he awaken me to go with him?"

"Maybe Alex and Nicolae took him by force."

"They were mighty quiet about it if they did. I'm not a heavy sleeper." He looked out in the direction of the darkened city. "I think that long nap yesterday afternoon really got the prince rested up. He's back to his old cocky self again—started to grumble about the confinement and mentioned he wanted to sample some of the Western night life."

We looked at each other silently in the faint illumination coming from the next boat.

"We've got to find him before it's too late. Are there any waterfront saloons within walking distance?" I asked, knowing full well Staghorn probably knew as little about Saint Louis as I did.

120

"Can't see any from here, but I'd guess there are. Probably tucked back among some o' those big warehouses and factories."

"Let's go check them out. Have you still got my gun?"

"Right here."

He slipped the walnut butt of the heavy Colt into my hand, and I holstered the pistol. I held up my hand for silence and caution as we started down the forward stairway to the main deck. Sleeping forms were huddled everywhere. We crept cautiously to the rail on the main deck. The big mate was nowhere to be seen. I couldn't distinguish the deckhands from the sleeping passengers. About halfway back on the port side I could see two forms moving in the darkness—apparently ministering to the sick.

Since no one had attempted to get ashore since the riot the police had withdrawn all but one of their men, who remained on guard each night. But more often than not, he could be seen drinking coffee with the mate on one of our adjoining boats.

Our landing stages were still up, but we climbed the guards and dropped softly to the edge of the water where it met the cobblestones in the deep shadows. In case anyone was watching, we crept along under the bows of the next three boats before starting up the long slope toward the row of dark buildings.

"Hope there aren't any police patrolling this waterfront," Fin panted as we paused in the shelter of a big brick building. "They made it pretty plain after that riot that anyone else trying to get off that quarantined boat would be jailed."

"To hell with that now. Which way?"

"Your guess is as good as mine."

We ducked into the first street we saw and walked down the middle of the deserted street in the pitch blackness between buildings. I jumped involuntarily at the sound of something scurrying in the darkness.

"I'll bet they've got rats down here big enough to carry you off," Staghorn whispered. "Some of those South American ports sure had 'em. There was a lot o' garbage in the streets to draw 'em."

We came to a cross street and went on to the next block. We were into the third block before we saw some sign of life. OTTO'S TAVERN proclaimed the sign over the open door. Light and noise was streaming out into the humid night.

The light was blinding when we entered the room. The sound of voices dropped as the men turned to look at us. In a few seconds I could see, and I sidled around the wall, vying to look inconspicuous, and failing, as all eyes except those of a few drunks followed us to the bar. The place was full of rough-looking men in work clothes. Plainly, this was a neighborhood saloon and not one frequented by strangers. Since it was almost 1:00 A.M., I was surprised at the crowd until I realized that this was Saturday night.

I briefly described to the bartender the three men we were looking for, but the big, rawboned man shook his head and shrugged. We thanked him and left quickly.

We had the same luck in four more saloons. I popped open my watch as we paused at a streetcorner under a gaslight. "Nearly two o'clock. Looks like we guessed wrong."

"Maybe he hailed a hack and went farther into town," Fin suggested.

"If so, we'll never find him. Did he mention having any connections in this city?"

"None."

"We might as well head back to the boat before we're missed. He may already be back."

We had wandered back and forth until we were about six city blocks from the waterfront. The streets were nearly deserted. Two drunks went weaving past us, trying to negotiate the uneven brick sidewalk. An occasional closed carriage rolled by, the horse's hooves clopping hollowly on the cobblestones.

Just as we stepped off the curb, a gunshot crashed somewhere ahead of us. Before the sound had time to die away, two more shots followed. As the explosions echoed off the buildings, I could hear feet running on pavement.

"Let's go!"

"Hellfire, Fin, what for? That's not our trouble. You're not even armed, and you want to run right into the middle of some gunfight or robbery? You're like some old fighter who jumps at the sound of a bell."

"It might be the prince in trouble."

I realized that he might be right. The last thing I wanted was a gunfight, but there was no backing off now. "Slim chance, but let's go see," I said.

We took off at a dead run toward the noise. There were no more shots, so we had only a general idea of where the sound had come from. We threw ourselves against the brick wall of the first building on the next block and eased up to look down the narrow alley beside it. I could hear nothing but my own breathing and my heart pounding in my ears. I slid over, Colt in hand, and put one eye around the corner. The alley was dark, and only a dim light showed where it opened onto the next street.

Two more shots blasted the quiet night.

123

"The next block. C'mon!"

Staghorn and I sprinted down the darkened alley and dashed recklessly across, through the illumination of a streetlamp, and into the next alleyway. A tongue of flame lashed out of the blackness. I heard the explosion, followed closely by the whine of a bullet off the wall somewhere behind us. We both dove face-first and slid on the slimy cobblestones. Without knowing who I was shooting at, I thumbed back the hammer of the Colt and let fly. Then I rolled toward the wall, away from my muzzle flash. Two more shots boomed in the narrow alley, but they were shooting as blindly as I was, and the bullets ricocheted harmlessly away. I fired again at the flashes, but apparently with no effect. Then I heard the sound of at least two men running toward the other end of the alley.

"Fin! You okay?" I whispered hoarsely. I could see nothing.

"Yeah. Right here."

The sound of the feet was growing fainter, but I caught a quick glimpse of two figures disappearing around the corner at the end of the alley about a hundred yards away.

I holstered my gun and stood up, wiping my hands on my pants. "No point in chasing them. The way they're moving, we'd never catch them this side of the river."

"Might walk into another ambush, too," Staghorn added. "Let's circle around the next block, just to be safe, before we go back."

Getting back aboard our quarantined boat, unseen, proved harder than getting ashore. The sound of the gunfire had brought some of the insomniacs and crew members from several of the steamboats out on deck. As we crouched by a loading dock, a black police paddy wagon clattered over the stones from one of the darkened streets along the landing. The rig came toward us for a hundred yards or so, and then the uniformed driver turned his horse back toward the city and disappeared into the shadows, apparently looking for the source of the shots.

There was no one near the *Silver Swan,* and we could see no movement aboard, but we circled about a half-mile above it before coming out of the shadows and across the stone landing to the line of moored boats. Then we walked as quietly as possible around and under the bows and guards of the various craft until we approached our own boat. We crouched under the bow of the next boat for at least ten minutes and watched for any sign of activity. Apparently everyone on this end was asleep. On a silent signal from me, we both crept up to the overhanging bow and jumped up to grab the stanchions of the rail to pull ourselves up. Staghorn got up first and reached down to help me.

"Well, as I live and breathe, here's two more."

My hair stood on end at the sound of the deep voice only a few feet away. But then I recognized it as belonging to Big John Wells.

"For a quarantined boat, there sure has been a lot of traffic back and forth ashore tonight," he continued as we climbed over the rail.

"You're not going to turn us in, are you?" Fin asked.

"Hell, no! That'd just mean more trouble and more delays. There's no need to say anything, since none o' you who've been ashore have had the sickness."

"Who's been ashore tonight besides us?" I asked.

"As far as I know just you two and the prince and a couple o' his men. I was in my bunk when all o' you took it in your heads to jump ship, or I'd'a'sure put a stop to it. Didn't think there was no need to post a watch, but I guess I was wrong."

"Where are they now?" I broke in.

"Who?"

"The prince and his men."

"I don't know. They went topside about ten minutes ago."

We left the mate still grumbling and bounded up the forward stairs.

The grand saloon was deserted, and the few lamps still burning were turned low. We made straight for the prince's stateroom and yanked the door open. Prince Zarahoff looked up sharply from his seat on the bed, apparently caught in mid-sentence with two of his men.

"Come in," he said.

We stepped inside and closed the door, taking in the scene before us. The left sleeve of the prince's white shirt was soaked with blood. The sleeve was ripped to the shoulder and Nicolae was swabbing a deep gash. Alex was pouring drinks for the three of them at a side table.

"What's going on?" I demanded, unable to think of anything else to say.

"Someone shot me," the prince replied. As I moved closer, I noticed the glassy look in his eyes and caught the pungent smell of brandy. I couldn't tell if he was slightly drunk or had just lost a lot of blood—or both.

"Do these men understand English?" Fin asked, indicating Nicolae and Alex.

"Only very little."

I didn't know what to do next. I wondered where the other two were. Were they asleep in the next room?

"If you wanted to go ashore, why didn't you wake me?" Fin demanded hotly, as if talking to a spoiled

126

child. "Hell, you could've gotten yourself killed out there. I thought I was supposed to be your bodyguard."

"I got bored," he replied simply. "I wanted to see one of your American Western saloons and gaming halls I heard so much about. I knew you would object." He shook his head. "It was not at all what I expected. No saloon girls. Very dull. Full of peasants drinking ale."

I almost smiled at this as I pictured him in the same type of workingman's tavern we had seen.

"What about these two?" I asked, indicating the hulking Rumanians, who were always strangely silent in our presence.

"Ah . . ." he replied, his glassy eyes growing brighter, "the only excitement of the night came as I was returning to the boat. Someone tried to shoot me from the darkness. Alex and Nicolae came along just in time to drive them off."

"Did you see who it was?"

Staghorn and I leaned forward intently for his answer as he cringed at the alcohol Nicolae was sponging into the raw gash.

"No. Only some figures moving in the shadows. One of their first shots hit me, but I ducked out of the way between some buildings and returned a few shots of my own," he added proudly. I noticed his clothes were streaked and grimed as if he had been rolling on the street.

"You didn't hear any voices or see any faces?" Fin asked.

"No. But I believe there were at least two of them."

I didn't look at them directly, but I could feel the eyes of Nicolae and Alex boring into me. I got the feeling they understood a lot more than they let on.

"It is very fortunate for you," I said slowly, looking

directly at the two Rumanians, "that these two came along. Do they have any idea who it was, or why someone would be shooting at you?"

"I questioned them about that," the prince replied. "My attackers got away without showing their faces. Alex thinks he may have wounded one of them." The prince shrugged slightly. "Robbers, probably. It might have been someone in the saloon who saw me and knew I had some gold." He flexed his left arm. "I don't believe this slight wound will hamper my movements after a few days. I should be perfectly fit by the time we hunt the great buffalo."

"If you went ashore alone, what were these two doing there?" I asked.

"They followed me ashore. They were concerned for my safety."

"Well, so was I, but I didn't know where you'd gone. How did they?" Staghorn asked.

"They were playing cards in the main cabin as I went out, and I told them where I was going. But I cautioned them to stay here, and make sure I wasn't missed. Now I'm glad they decided to follow me."

Fin and I looked at each other.

"What the hell do you think we've been doing for the past two hours—out walking for our health?" Fin asked. "We went ashore looking for you, too. And got ourselves shot at—probably by the same two who were after you." He pointed at the two Rumanians. "How do you know it wasn't these two who tried to kill you?" he demanded, voicing what both of us were thinking.

Anger darkened the prince's groggy countenance. "You will *not* slander the reputation of my men in my presence!" he snapped. "I know of your suspicions, but they are totally unfounded. If it hadn't been for Alex and Nicolae, I could very well be dead of some outlaw's bullet right now. The men are completely loyal to me."

"Well, if that's the way you feel about it, then maybe you'd better get yourself another American bodyguard!" Fin retorted, his face reddening as he jerked the door open. "Or, you can leave yourself in the hands of these two—and wind up a corpse before you ever see Omaha!"

The short, muscular Alex and the big, rough-handed Nicolae stared at us impassively, showing neither surprise, fear, nor anger as we went out into the saloon and closed the door behind us. How much of this exchange they had understood, I had no way of knowing.

"Well, the cat's out of the bag now," I commented as we headed for our staterooms. "If they didn't know they were prime suspects before, we just erased all doubt."

"I'm glad to wash my hands of the whole thing," Fin said. "If everyone in Rumania is as mule-headed as that prince, it's no wonder they have political problems."

"Maybe so," I countered. "But if you were in a foreign country and one of the natives accused your traveling companions of trying to kill you, but presented no evidence or motive, what would you think?"

He paused with his hand on the brass knob of his stateroom door. "You've got a point. I never thought of it that way. Oh, well, the responsibility's off my shoulders now. G'dnight, Matt."

CHAPTER 13

THE FOLLOWING DAY WAS SUNDAY. SINCE THERE WAS no place we could go, even to church, I tried to sleep late, but the muggy heat drove me out of bed by 8:30.

My eyeballs were gritty from too little sleep. Because of the holiday, there was not even the usual loading and unloading of cargo and the clattering drays on the landing to watch.

"Much more of this, and a man could become an alcoholic, just for lack of something better to do," Wiley remarked to me as we sat in captain's chairs outside our rooms, listening to the far-off chiming of church bells in the city.

I was so tired I could think of no appropriate answer. I had already filled him in on our adventure of the night before. "That's one scrape you can't blame on me," had been his retort. "I'm glad you didn't wake me."

About midafternoon, the Saint Louis doctor wheeled up in an open buggy, and a landing stage was lowered to allow him aboard. He stayed about an hour, most of the time on the main deck. We were all used to his visits and paid little attention until he appeared on the cabin deck and started aft toward the ladies' section, accompanied by Captain Wilson. Several of the passengers looked up idly from reading or conversation as they passed. Wiley, Fin, and I put down our poker hands and looked significantly at each other as the doctor paused at a door and rapped. The door opened, and he and the captain disappeared inside.

"That's Ellen Vivrette's room." With that simple statement, Wiley voiced the dread that suddenly clutched at all of us.

It was only a matter of minutes before they reappeared, accompanied by the older couple—Ellen's family friends—who had been unable to leave the boat at Cairo for their return to Louisville. The captain walked briskly ahead as they crossed again through the grand saloon, followed by the doctor and the older

130

couple, who were supporting between them a girl I hardly recognized at first glance. Ellen's face was drawn and pale. In spite of the heat, she was wrapped in a shawl and seemed to be shivering. She looked very weak, but was making a valiant effort to walk.

"What do you reckon is wrong with her?" Wiley asked as the party passed us.

"Maybe worked herself into the grippe," Fin guessed.

"Either that or she caught the cholera herself."

"Oh, no!" Wiley paled slightly.

"I guess that's the reason we haven't seen her the last day or two."

"Every time I tried to see her lately, her friends told me she was in her cabin, resting, and shouldn't be disturbed," Wiley said. He jumped up and caught the group as they neared the end of the grand saloon. "What is it? What's wrong with her, Doc? Is it the cholera?" He could barely keep his voice from rising.

The doctor shook off Wiley's hand impatiently, glancing around at several of the cabin passengers who were watching. "No. This is no concern of yours. This girl has just eaten something that doesn't agree with her."

The party continued out the door and down the stairs, leaving Wiley staring. Ellen had never looked up.

We all went out on the port-side deck to watch as the doctor, Ellen, and her friends went down the landing stage to shore. They were followed closely by several of the crewman and immigrants helping the cholera patients from the main deck or carrying them on litters. While we were inside, six ambulances had drawn up nearby, and it was into these that all the sick were placed. Some of those who were able sat up, four or six to the vehicle. The ambulance doors were closed, and the drivers slapped their reins and pulled away in line.

"It's the cholera. I'm sure of it," Wiley said grimly. "Wonder what hospital they're taking them to?" Worry lines creased his forehead.

"The doc said it was something she ate," Fin said. "You don't think she might have been poisoned, too?"

"The doctor lied," Wiley stated flatly.

Nobody replied.

"Sir?" I looked around at the steward who was touching my arm. "The captain is going to make an announcement. He'd like all the passengers to gather in the saloon."

We drifted back inside as the rest of the cabin passengers assembled to hear Captain Wilson, who was climbing up on a table to make himself seen and heard.

"Ladies and gentlemen," Captain Wilson began when the saloon was more than half-full, "let me have your attention, please!" The murmur of voices gradually died. "I'm happy to announce that our enforced detention is nearly at an end."

There was scattered applause and a vigorous nodding of heads.

"The city authorities have informed me that those of you who are continuing on upriver, those going up the Missouri or going back south to other ports on the Ohio may leave the *Silver Swan* at any time. However, you will be escorted directly to your various boats or trains; you may not enter Saint Louis. The same holds for our deck passengers. There is a fear that the cholera will somehow spread into the city if these precautions are not taken. Those of you who are ending your journey here at Saint Louis will be obliged to spend another ten days of quarantine aboard the *Silver Swan*. The crew and I will do all in our power to make your enforced detention as pleasant as possible."

There was a mixed reaction to this: some consternation, some relief. The crowd broke up, some of them heading directly to their staterooms, to pack. Strident voices were raised as part of the crowd gathered around the captain.

"Why do you suppose they're changing their minds and letting people off now?" Fin asked. The three of us moved away from the noise.

"I guess since some of the passengers have already escaped into town, the city fathers want to get rid of as many of the rest of us as they can to avoid another panic," I answered. "Either that, or they've just had a change of heart."

Some of the passengers left the boat immediately, including many of the immigrants from the main deck. We got our things together, glad to be finally free of this boat, its problems, and the pestilence. The three of us had our through tickets, purchased in New Orleans, to Bismarck, connecting to the Benton Line here in Saint Louis. Since we had already been delayed so long, we had no idea if the *Western,* the boat we were booked on, was even in Saint Louis, so we were in no hurry.

We ate a good lunch in the saloon, finished packing our gear, and went down to the main deck. It seemed strange to be leaving—almost like moving away from a place we had lived for a long time. We had been on the *Silver Swan* only a few days, but, with everything that had happened, it seemed like much longer. We shook hands with Big John Wells, and he wished us well. I was sorry to see the last of the big mate. He had proven himself a real friend and was always there when we needed him.

We walked up the levee, looking for any Benton Line

boat since we had been told the *Western* had already departed. A uniformed policeman kept pace with us at a distance to be sure we didn't leave the waterfront.

Almost a half-mile above we came upon two almost identical vessels, the *Nellie Peck* and the *Yankton,* both J. C. Power boats. THE BENTON LINE was painted in black letters just below the wide pilothouse window of each boat. We chose the *Yankton* because it happened to be the first one we came to, and went aboard. We hunted up the clerk and presented our tickets. He checked his passenger list and found that he had several vacant rooms. The boat was scheduled to depart on Monday morning, and the passenger list was not full, so he honored our tickets through to Bismarck. The boat's ultimate destination was Fort Benton, Montana Territory, the head of navigation on the Missouri River. We carried our duffles to our small rooms and went to look over the rest of our new home. We found it small, plain, and drab compared to what we had just left. It was like climbing off a Pullman car into a buckboard. The sturdy little mountain boat was a stern-wheeler, about two hundred feet long, with a main cabin only about eighteen feet wide and flanked by the cabin doors. It had a bare pine floor, and three two-oil-lamp chandeliers—no Persian carpet, no grand piano, no silver coffee urn. The craft was built for rugged work. It didn't take us long to circle the entire boat. The main deck was already loaded to capacity with boxes, barrels, and sacks of every description—flour, whiskey, bitters, canned goods, clothing, wagon wheels, and other manufactured goods consigned upriver to the various army posts and remote towns of the Montana gold fields. The deck space that wasn't already filled with cargo was stacked high with cordwood for the boilers.

We finally climbed to the hurricane deck and up the steps to the empty pilothouse. Though not as grand or as high above the river as the wheelhouse of the *Silver Swan,* the glass on all four sides provided a good view of the boat and everything surrounding it.

"I wonder if it's too late to cash in our tickets and catch a train going west?" I wondered aloud, glancing out over the brass-studded spokes of the big wheel between the two tall smokestacks.

"You wouldn't want to miss seeing what will happen on the rest of this trip, now, would you?" Wiley asked. "Take a look at who's coming along." He pointed out the front window at a group of men standing by the gangway, talking and gesturing. It was Prince Zarahoff and his four retainers.

"Well, this might prove to be a more interesting voyage than I expected," I said.

Neither Wiley nor Fin replied as we watched the five come up the landing stage and disappear below us onto the main deck.

"Wonder why they selected this boat?"

"They probably had through tickets just like we did. And the Power and the Coulson Lines are about the only regular steamboat lines running the upper Missouri now."

"Strange they would choose this boat over the *Nellie Peck* or one of the other boats, though."

I shrugged. "Probably the first Power Company boat they came to," I said, glancing at the big P suspended prominently between the two black chimneys. "Just like we did."

"Can't say as I want to be on the same boat with the prince," Fin said. "He draws bad luck."

"You're not one of those superstitious sailors, are

you?" Wiley asked as we pushed open the door and went down the steps to the hurricane deck.

"Not superstitious," he replied. "But some people just seem to draw trouble. And he's one of them."

Some of the same Irish and Norwegian immigrants were crowded aboard as deck passengers. I couldn't figure out how they would find room to lie down at night along with the roustabouts. Every square foot of space would have to be used. I had seen many of the deck passengers on the *Silver Swan* bedding down on crates and bales.

I had watched the prince's party come aboard with strange misgivings—almost akin to a premonition. Even though our accommodations aboard this mountain packet were comfortable and spacious by comparison to a coach or train, I had the feeling that I would rather be continuing this trip overland, free from Prince Zarahoff and his party.

"Why hasn't the prince been met and escorted in style from place to place by some dignitary?" I inquired as we descended the stairs to the main saloon. "Instead, he's scrambling for space aboard this boat like the rest of us commoners."

"I wondered the same thing," Wiley replied. "He told me he didn't want any royal treatment. Remember what he told us the night of the fight when he came to our room? Said he wanted to experience this wild frontier America just like any other traveler—at least until he meets up with Buffalo Bill at Bismarck."

"Then there'll be a show," I said. "Buffalo Bill Cody does things in style. Everybody in the country will know a Rumanian prince is here."

"That's for sure," Wiley agreed. "He's a born showman, if there ever was one. Sometimes puts P. T.

Barnum in the shade."

"Speaking of letting everyone know the prince is here, I just had an idea," I said. "If I could get into town tomorrow before this boat sails, maybe I could work up a deal with the Saint Louis *Globe-Democrat* to sell them my story of the prince's trip—say, a good, intimate human interest angle."

"Think what a great story it would make if you could write about attempted murder," Wiley said.

"And then write a happy ending to it when the would-be assassins are caught," Fin finished.

"If they *are* ever caught," Wiley said. "*And* if they don't succeed."

"It's all wishful thinking anyway," I concluded. "They won't let me into town, and this boat is sailing in the morning."

"Hell, write it anyway," Fin urged. "You'll be able to sell it to somebody. It doesn't have to be the *Globe-Democrat*.*"

"Not a bad idea. I'll start on it tonight. I may have to pump the prince for some more personal information. Don't know why I didn't think of it before. Maybe my reporter's instincts are slipping. Or else I was just too caught up in the action."

"Speaking of newspapers, there's a boy on the landing selling them," Wiley said. "Hey, boy! Up here. Paper!" he yelled. The boy bounded toward the gangway in anticipation of a sale and Wiley went to meet him. He was back in a minute, handing us each several sheets of the paper. Here, at least, was something to relieve the boredom.

I had swapped sections with Fin and was scanning one of the back pages when an article caught my eye. I read it quickly, and then went back and read it again with more care. The details were sketchy, but it reported that a man had been found shot to death in an alley near the waterfront the night before. His killer was unknown, but identification in his pockets indicated his name was Ronald Whitlaw of Quincy, Illinois. Robbery was apparently not the motive, since he had about $40 in his pockets. The name and the general description of the body teased a recollection at the back of my mind. But when the reporter speculated that the man might have been a recent passenger on one of the riverboats, the memory hit me. It was the broken-toothed man who had attacked me for breaking up the fight and had threatened me the next day, attempting to force $500 out of me for the gambling losses for himself and his well-dressed friend.

"Men, I think the prince was telling the truth."

"About what?" Fin asked.

"You remember what he said last night about his two men coming along just in time to drive off some would-be robbers?"

"Yeah."

"And that Alex thought he had wounded one of them? Well, the body of a man from the *Silver Swan* was found shot to death in an alley near where we were last night. He was the same man who led the attack on me the night of the fight. And the same one who threatened me about getting his money back—Ron Whitlaw."

"Hell, it might have been one of us who shot him," Fin said.

"Possibly. But this man struck me as being capable of most anything. He probably had his eye on the prince and followed him ashore, thinking he'd be easy pickings—and worth a lot more than I was. Our theory about the prince's men being at the root of his attempted murder may be all wet."

We looked at each other blankly. Our carefully thoughtout premise seemed to be coming apart.

We got up and wandered through the small saloon. The prince and his four men were moving their luggage into two rooms almost opposite ours. The prince looked our way, but made no sign of recognition; he went right on telling his men where to stow his voluminous luggage. His left shoulder was heavily bandaged under his shirt, and he seemed to be moving his left arm with some difficulty.

"A strange man," Fin remarked as we went back through our rooms to lounge and smoke in the deck chairs outside.

"Probably the result of a pretty strange unbringing," Wiley said, "at least by our standards. The idea of the divine right of kings may be long gone, but kings and dictators still consider themselves several cuts above the ordinary mortal—especially the crude peasants living on the frontier of a wilderness." He grinned and raked a match across the bottom of his wooden chair to light his slim cigar.

After we finished the newspaper, we sat and talked for an hour or so, trying to distract ourselves from the shimmering waves of heat that rose from the landing and enveloped us in a windless blanket of humidity.

I noticed that Wiley was taking less and less part in the conversation. He was staring off toward the city, apparently preoccupied.

"You know, looking back on it, we were damned lucky to have escaped that cholera," Fin said when the conversation drifted around to the disease.

"We may not be out of the woods yet," I reminded him. "We, or any of these deck passengers from the *Silver Swan,* could be carrying it."

"Speaking of cholera," Wiley said, apparently taking note of the conversation for the first time in several minutes, "I wonder what hospital they took those patients to?"

"You mean, 'Where did they take Ellen Vivrette?' " I said.

"Yes," he acknowledged. "That's it. I've been thinking seriously of staying over to see how she's getting along. We got to be pretty good friends the short time I knew her."

"They'd never let you into town."

"No matter. I'd find a way to slip in and see her."

"Her friends are with her. She said she was coming here to visit a cousin, so she probably has kin with her now. What good do you think you can do?"

"None. Maybe just help her morale. Let her know that somebody cares."

"I've seen you moon-struck before," I said at the risk of raising his ire, "and it usually fades out about as fast as it comes on. You've only known this girl a few days."

A pained look came into his eyes, and he looked away from me. "It was her willingness to help other people that attracted me, aside from her obvious charms. She took on a job nobody else wanted. She volunteered to put herself in danger to help relieve the sufferings of people she didn't even know."

I had no comeback for that.

"You never know a person until you see that person under stress. I feel I've known her a lot longer than a few days, since I've seen her under pressure, as well as socially." Wiley paused and grinned. "But you're right; my heart does overrule my head a good bit of the time."

"You're really considering staying, then?" I asked.

140

He nodded. "This girl is something special. If I leave now, I may never see her again. And I would always wonder if our relationship could have developed into something more. Besides"—he smiled, suddenly aware of his serious tone—"I always was a sucker for a pretty face."

"You're hopeless," I laughed. "You're really just a homebody at heart and are looking to settle down and get married."

He looked uncomfortable. "Well, I've made up my mind—if for no other reason than to satisfy my curiosity. I may be on the next boat upriver, but I think I'll go look up the clerk and cash in my ticket."

He got up and went into our room, as if afraid that further conversation with us might weaken his decision to stay.

CHAPTER 14

IT WAS JUST AFTER FULL DAYLIGHT THE NEXT MORNING when the *Yankton*, with a blast on her steam whistle, threw off her mooring lines and backed into the Mississippi, leaving Wiley Jenkins somewhere ashore. He had gone quietly down the landing stage after dark the night before, his canvas bag of belongings slung over one arm. He had gripped our hands in an emotional farewell and promised, one way or another, by train or coach, to meet us at one of the upper Missouri ports, possibly before we reached Bismarck. "If you need to contact me, just send a letter to General Delivery at the main post office," he said over his shoulder as he left.

Even though our new boat was much smaller and cruder than the opulent *Silver Swan*, its cooks served up a surprisingly good breakfast.

"I guess we were just spoiled by the *Silver Swan*," Fin Staghorn remarked. "But that was an artificial world. Guess we need to be brought back to reality gradually."

We walked out onto the deck just in time to see the junction of the Missouri coming up.

The boat slowed and swung expertly into mid-channel to turn wide into the main current of the Big Muddy. And an apt name it was. The milky-colored water of the smaller river poured into the dark greenish gray of the Mississippi, but the lighter water did not mix or dissipate immediately. The Missouri's water flowed along inshore, forming a separate stream, a wide streak, for several miles downstream toward Saint Louis.

The river looked fairly full as we swung into it. The mud and sand flats on each shoreline were minimal. Rows of pilings set out from each bank at intervals indicated that the Army Corps of Engineers had been at work trying to tame this part of the wild Missouri. There were no other boats in sight, and the deserted river gave no hint that the old river town of Saint Charles was only a short distance upriver. Within moments after we steamed into the Missouri and started west I felt as if we were entering a whole different world.

The staterooms of the *Yankton* were even smaller than the ones on the *Silver Swan*; so, even though Wiley had departed, Fin and I decided to maintain our adjacent, but separate, quarters to give ourselves some elbow room. Each room contained a single wooden bedstead, a table and chair, and room for nothing else.

Besides the prince and his men, who occupied two larger rooms, the other twenty-odd cabin passengers consisted of five army officers and their wives, seven or eight merchants or drummers, and an odd assortment of roughly dressed men who could have been anything

142

from miners to laborers. One man, who kept strictly to himself, wore the well-used buckskins of a frontiersman or scout. The prince's party and several of the deck passengers we had recognized were the only people besides ourselves from the *Silver Swan* who were continuing upriver on the *Yankton*.

We made a short stop at Saint Charles, apparently to take on fuel for the fireboxes. No passengers got off or on, and there was no room for more freight. No one had time to get impatient before we cast off, slid beneath the railroad bridge, and steamed on upriver.

"Where are these immigrants headed?" I asked Fin as we stood after supper near the capstans on the lower deck watching the sun fade into an orange ball over the tree line off our port bow and enjoying the slight breeze our motion was creating.

He shrugged. "Not sure. Usually the Irish settle in the cities. Some o' these aren't new immigrants. They may be going to take jobs on the railroad. The Norwegians are probably homesteading or heading up for work on the harvest in a few weeks. Every Norwegian I've ever met who wasn't following the sea was land-hungry. Farmland is scarce in Norway, so a lot of them are forced to the sea as fishermen or deepwater seamen to make a living."

We turned to watch the deckhands who were off duty, lounging on some of the wooden boxes, talking and smoking. A few of the immigrants were sharing their meager rations. The grub pile aboard this boat was not nearly as sumptuous as that aboard the *Silver Swan*. The first mate of the *Yankton* was a smaller man than Big John but was compact and muscular and depended on a stentorian voice and a .38 Smith & Wesson to maintain authority over his knife-wielding roustabouts. The mate had a tiny sleeping room of his own on the cabin deck and presently was nowhere to be seen.

"While things are quiet, I think I'll get started on that story," I remarked at length. But I made no move to get up from my perch on one of the bitts; the evening was just too pleasant to go inside yet. Except for the explosive booming of the steam-escape pipes aft, we were far removed from the noise of the machinery and the showers of tiny cinders from the smokestacks. I could hear a rushing sound as a continuous sheet of muddy water peeled away from our saucer-shaped bow. The dark green trees along the bluffs on either side of the river were growing darker as dusk came on. It seemed that our boat was the only intrusion into this peaceful world of nature that was settling down for sleep. I hoped this tranquillity would last the rest of the trip, but I had an underlying premonition that it was only an interlude of calm. Even if no further trouble occurred with the prince, Wiley Jenkins and Fin Staghorn had both warned me that even the most routine riverboat trip was not without its perils and excitement. How well I could attest to that so far!

I glanced up toward the pilothouse, but it was too far aft to see from where we sat on the bow. The only thing visible was the top half of the tall, black chimneys that were pouring thick plumes of smoke into the darkening sky. We had explored our new floating world during the day and found that she contained 28 cabin passengers, about 35 deck passengers, 20 or so roustabouts, 2 pilots, a clerk and 2 cooks, 2 cabin boys, 2 firemen, 2 engineers, a chambermaid, a carpenter, and 2 mates. On a boat this size there was less formality since everyone had to live within a few feet of each other for weeks on end. Social distinctions tended to blur, even though a sharp division still existed between cabin and deck passengers.

A slowing of the paddle wheel indicated we were putting into shore to tie up for the night. Only during periods of high water and a full moon did Missouri River pilots dare risk their vessels against the snags and shoals and tricky current. Several roustabouts came forward to handle the lines as the *Yankton* nosed carefully toward the wooded bank. Fin and I moved out of their way, and Fin slapped his bare arm.

"Damned mosquitoes going to be bad tonight," he remarked. "It'll be pretty stuffy with all the doors and windows closed."

We climbed the forward stairs to the cabin deck and strolled aft to our rooms. I excused myself and retired, eager to get started on my story. I had not done any writing since selling a feature article several weeks before to my old newspaper, the Chicago *Times-Herald,* about the capture of the stage-robbery gang in the Black Hills. Even though it was not an exclusive, the paper paid me well for my firsthand account. I felt an urge to get back to my writing.

I lighted and turned up the coal-oil lamp in its wall sconce, dug out a bottle of ink and a couple of steel-tipped pens from my luggage. The small wooden table served as a writing desk, and its single drawer contained some stationery that was engraved at the top:

BENTON P LINE
Steamer YANKTON

Just below this was a faithful rendering of the boat itself in the form of an ink drawing. I arranged the paper and my thoughts, opened the ink bottle, and began. My pen scratched late into the night as the June bugs popped and buzzed against the glass of the half-opened transom over my outside door. But before I shoved the sheets into my leather dispatch case and turned in, I had put down a fairly accurate rough draft of our adventures with Prince Zarahoff, the cholera, and the *Silver Swan* from New Orleans up to the present. At least the story had been captured on paper before any of the pertinent details slipped my mind, I thought with satisfaction as I slid under the single cotton sheet and settled myself for sleep.

The cruise quickly shook down into a routine as we crossed the state of Missouri. We plowed against the current all day, staying in the channel and negotiating the tricky bends. At dark we tied up for the night, the boilers were drained, and the ends removed so a roustabout could crawl inside to shovel out the steaming mud—a daily reminder of the load of silt this river was carrying.

We ate our meals in the main cabin with the other passengers, including the cabin crew and the officers who weren't on watch.

We spoke or nodded to Prince Zarahoff whenever we encountered him strolling the deck or at meals, or playing cards in the main cabin with his four men who seldom left his side. He was formally courteous but cool toward us. Possibly it was just my imagination; perhaps it was just an imperious aloofness that was part of his nature and was not intended to be unfriendly.

To make the trip more interesting, Fin and I struck up an aquaintance with Will Hosey, one of the two pilots. He was a man in his early forties with fair skin, and reddish hair and mustache that were graying slightly. He was about five ten with a solid build and muscular forearms. We discovered he had held a master's certificate for sixteen years. When we expressed an interest in the finer points of piloting, and he found out Fin was a deepwater sailor, he invited us to join him in the wheelhouse when he went on duty that afternoon. We didn't need a second invitation.

"Howdy, gents," he greeted us about two hours later as we entered the open door of the wheelhouse. He glanced around at us briefly, and then his eyes went immediately back to the river before him. "Glad you decided to join me." He sounded sincerely glad for the company. "Have a seat on the bench back there if you've a mind."

"I think I'll stand," I replied.

"Your pleasure." He let fly a brown stream of tobacco juice at a big brass cuspidor nearby and hit it dead center—apparently the result of long practice. He eased the wheel down a few spokes, wiped his mustache, then moved back to stand directly behind the big, brass-bound wooden steering wheel. Even though it was sunk to its hub in the deck, it still stood up a good four and a half feet.

"River looks to be pretty full," Fin commented.

"Yeh, but she's droppin' by the hour," was the dour reply. "By rights, this shouldn't be called a river atall—more like a muddy sink that floods a couple of times a year, when she ain't froze. Too thick to drink, too thin to plow." Another spurt of tobacco juice scored a hit in the spittoon.

In spite of his words, I got the feeling that he wasn't so much damning the Missouri as he was subtly bragging of his skill in negotiating it. As he spoke, he was never completely still. He sidled from one side of the wheel to the other, giving or taking a few spokes, his eyes sweeping the panorama before us, picking up some memorized marks—a bluff here, a point there—reading the current, calculating the position of a towhead or a hidden bar. As he worked, he continued talking and using the spittoon regularly. But his eyes never left the river. "See that set o' antlers out there?" He jabbed a thumb toward the front window. I looked at the magnificent elk horns affixed to the top of the pilothouse just above the glass. "Yeah."

"Those are awarded to the fastest boat in the company fleet. The *Yankton* has 'em now for our run last year from Bismarck to Benton in eleven days and one hour."

Fin whistled. "That's fast! Were you the pilot?"

"One of 'em. Josiah Vaughn was the other one. We had a helluva, run. Plenty of water under our bottom. Did some night running with a full moon and good weather all the way. Couldn't have done it otherwise. We hit it lucky. There's a lot of luck involved in setting any kind of speed record. Everything has to fall into place."

I saw a big, wooded island approaching. To the left of it the river dissipated in shallow meanderings over and around sandbars and snags of dead trees—clearly impassable. Most of the river's water seemed to be squeezed between the right-hand side of the island and the shoreline, forcing a rushing of muddy brown.

Hosey yanked a cord that hung near the right side of the pilothouse. A bell jangled. Then, keeping one hand on the wheel, he leaned over and flipped open the cap on a speaking tube. "Fred?"

"Yeah?" replied a voice faintly through the tube.

"Give me another wad of steam."

"Right, Captain."

In a few seconds the tempo of the machinery increased, and we could feel the vibrations through our feet.

148

"Are you the captain?" Fin asked, as Hosey pointed the *Yankton*'s bow at the narrow chute to the right of the island.

"Captain, part owner, and one of the pilots," he replied. "It's riskier than just working for good wages, but the rewards are a lot better when you have a good run."

I didn't want to interrupt, but I couldn't believe that he was going to try to take the boat up that narrow chute. Trees overhung the water on both sides, and there seemed to be no way a packet even as small as the *Yankton* could fit. I leaned against the port-side windows, Fin leaned against the starboard side, and we held our collective breath as the stocky pilot lined up our jackstaff on the center of the rushing torrent. Hosey fell silent as he concentrated on the job at hand.

Even though we were bucking a stiff current, the island seemed to be rushing at us with dizzying speed. The boat plunged right into the cleft, and I braced myself for the grinding crunch I knew would follow. The boat slowed as we met the resistance of the rushing water, but the deck vibrated as the high-pressure steam engines moved the boat steadily ahead. My heart jumped into my throat at the sound of crunching and snapping, but it was only the overhanging limbs of the trees brushing the sides of the boat at the boiler deck level. Hosey's eyes flickered from side to side. Just as the island's shoreline bent slightly, he spun the wheel down, caught it, held it steady for a few seconds. There was a slight bump that threw me forward as we touched the bank or bottom. Hosey brought the wheel up sharply, the shoreline fell away, and fifty yards later, we were in clear water.

"Whew!" I let out my breath in a rush and had to go

back and sit on the bench since my knees were feeling a little shaky.

"Nice work," Fin nodded. "Very nice. At sea you at least don't have obstacles like that to worry about."

"All in a day's work on this river," the pilot replied.

"I thought you were going to have to grease the sides of this packet to get her through that crack," I said.

Will Hosey chuckled. "That was our only way around that island," he said. "But it wasn't as reckless as it looked. I knew I had plenty of water. And the shoreline hasn't changed any that I could tell since I was last through there. If I was coming up on that for the first time, I'd have taken it a lot more cautiously."

I got up and stepped to the open back door of the wheelhouse for a breath of fresh air. The myriad small panes of glass in all four sides of the pilothouse afforded an unobstructed and impressive view of the river from this height, but they also let in a lot of hot sunlight. Besides the twisting river with its brown water and dun-colored sandbars, the surrounding countryside was green trees and grass, rock bluffs, and some cleared farmland showing beyond. Occasionally a farmhouse or the top of a barn appeared in the folds of the hills, and now and then a cow or horse could be seen grazing.

"Where are we, anyway?"

"Well, our last stop was at Hermann. We'll be coming up on Gasconade shortly. That's right where the Gasconade River flows in from the south. Beyond that is Jefferson City."

"The capital?"

"Right."

"Think we'll make that by dark?"

"Barring any problems we will." He jangled the bell and leaned over the speaking tube once more. "You can ease off on her now, Fred."

"Right, Captain," the engineer's voice answered. "Nice bit of steering, but you oughta see the clutter, o' leaves and limbs we got down here."

Hosey chuckled as he flipped the brass cap over the tube. "He swears I do that intentionally sometimes."

At this point the river was broad and straight for about a half-mile, so he let the boat have her head and relaxed a little. He glanced at Fin again. "I don't reckon it's any o' my business, but you look like you tangled with a grizzly—and lost."

Staghorn put his hand to his left cheekbone, which was still purple, but no longer swollen. His eye had come through undamaged. He smiled ruefully. "You should have seen it a few days ago. And you're about right; he hit like a grizzly even if he did use his head."

"His head? You wouldn't be referring to George Devol by any chance?"

"The same. You know him?"

"Seen him a few times, but know him mostly by reputation. He's been playing the rivers for years. But he sticks mostly to the lower Mississippi now. So you ran afoul of him, did you? Well, you're lucky you didn't come off with any worse damage."

The conversation ran on in this vein and then drifted to other river topics for the next hour or so. Finally, after rounding one of the many bends, the pilot identified the tiny hamlet of Gasconade coming up on the port side. He ordered the engines slowed to ease the boat in toward the landing. Even after the mooring hawsers were in place and one cargo boom was swinging barrels into a waiting wagon, there was nothing much to see here. Gasconade looked like just another sleepy little Missouri River town where the

151

greatest excitement was a Saturday night saloon brawl, or a dogfight, or the arrival of a steamboat.

Fin and I stepped down onto the hurricane deck to watch the unloading operation as the small, auxiliary steam engine was activated to operate the cargo boom. The steam engine was located in the hold just below the capstans on the bow. The cables run by this engine winched the boom up and around.

The operation was quick and smooth, and in no time the small crowd of townspeople at the landing was disappearing into the distance behind us as we started toward Jefferson City.

We climbed back into the pilothouse and smoked our pipes and chatted with Will Hosey for the next two hours. It was a pleasure to watch a real professional at work. He guided the big steamboat automatically, effortlessly, up the twisting, deceptive channel of the Missouri. His earlier statement that the river level was dropping by the hour may not have been an exaggeration. Even to my inexperienced eyes, the river seemed shallower, more spread out, and the sandbars more protruding with every tributary creek and river we passed.

The sun was creeping down the long western sky when Hosey remarked that Jefferson City was less than three miles away. The river was tending toward the northwest here, and the lowering sun to our left front was throwing up a fierce glare off the water's surface. Squinting out the front window of the wheelhouse, I could see practically nothing of the river before us. Hosey retrieved his hat from under the back bench it and pulled the brim low over his eyes in a vain attempt to shield his vision from the blinding rays reflecting upward.

A few seconds later he jumped for the speaking tube. "Fred! Cut the steam! Just leave me enough to give her steerageway."

The paddle wheel had been turning its normal twenty revolutions per minute since leaving Gasconade. But before Hosey could even straighten up again at the wheel, we were suddenly thrown forward as the boat came to a shuddering halt.

CHAPTER 15

"DAMN!" HOSEY SWORE, RECOVERING HIS BALANCE.

As I got up, rubbing my knee where I had banged it against the iron potbelly stove, I could feel the stroke of the engines and paddle wheel slowing. But it was too late.

Hosey brushed past us and was out the door and down the steps in two jumps. He ran to the forward end of the hurricane deck and peered intently over the low rail, walking back and forth to each side, trying to see how badly we were grounded.

"Hope we didn't hit a snag," Fin said. "Or we might have torn the bottom out of her."

"It felt pretty solid—like sand or mud," I answered.

"With this load of cargo and passengers, we're probably drawing a good four feet."

By the time we got down to the hurricane deck, the pilot was already below on the main deck at the bow while two roustabouts were jabbing poles over the sides, testing the depth of the water. A crowd of curious passengers was gathering to watch as Hosey studied the sluggish current and our position on the submerged bar.

The engineer reversed the wheel and gave it a shot of

steam. The paddle wheel tore at the water for a few minutes, driving water up under the hull and pulling backward at the same time. But it was to no avail. Hosey ordered the steam throttle shut down after a few minutes when the boat remained stuck fast.

"I think we can walk 'er across into deeper water. We hit soft mud and sand. No hull damage."

He gave a brief command to the mate standing nearby, and before he could even repeat the order, the roustabouts were jumping to rig the spars, as if by habit of long practice. It was a procedure I had only heard of, but never seen. Staghorn told me the boat he had come downriver on several years before had had to resort to this method of getting over some shallow bars. Sparring, or "grasshoppering," as it was called, consisted of using the cargo booms that stuck out like two giant antennae from the foredeck to swing out two spars, each about the size of a telegraph pole. The upper end of each spar was attached by blocks and cables to the end of the boom and the other end was dropped to the bottom of the river ahead of the boat at about a forty-five-degree angle. With mechanical leverage gained through a series of loops through blocks attached to the main deck and the top of the spar, the cable was wound in by means of the steam capstans. As the cables tightened, the forward half of the boat was literally lifted and the boat drawn forward before slamming down. The cables were loosened, the spars pulled up and swung forward, and the whole process repeated, until the boat was again afloat in deeper water.

"I hear on the upper reaches of the Missouri they sometimes have to row heavy lines ashore and attach them to trees and winch the boat ahead that way—just drag it across the shoals by main force," Fin remarked

154

as we watched the crew rig the spars. "And if even that won't do it, they have to off-load part of the cargo and come back for it later—'double-tripping,' they call it."

"No wonder it takes weeks and weeks to reach Fort Benton."

"Just one more reason the railroads are gradually taking over."

The mate waved the crowd back as the spars were positioned, and the capstans began to take up slack on the cable. From our position above on the hurricane deck, Fin and I had a perfect view of the operation. Prince Zarahoff and his men were among the crowd on the foredeck, watching. The prince apparently took offense at the way the mate ordered everyone away from the straining capstans. The mate, not knowing or caring who the prince was, gave him a shove when he didn't move immediately. The prince shoved the mate back and gave some retort I couldn't hear. They lunged at each other as the four Rumanians jumped in to pull them apart. Captain Hosey was already back up in the pilothouse and didn't see the scuffle break out. No damage was done as the two were separated and the mate shook himself free and walked off with a shrug. After a few words, the prince's retainers also retreated below us, leaving the royal visitor to stand close to the roustabouts and observe the unique operation of poling the big boat over the bar.

I could feel the boat begin to lift gradually under my feet until the bow was clear of the water. As the spars were drawn in by the cables, there was a breaking and groaning of the *Yankton*'s timbers as she was lifted bodily from the water. Then she rocked forward and slammed down in sheets of muddy spray. The roustabouts jumped forward and began to unwind the slackened cable as the spars tilted loosely forward along each side of the bow. The boat had "grasshoppered," literally hopping forward between its two long legs. The booms pulled the spars from the bottom as the paddle wheel slowed. Then the spars were swung forward again to repeat the process.

The boat creaked and groaned as the little steam engine strained to lift her a second time. Just as the bow began to come up, and the cables were at their greatest tension, I heard a loud pop and a whistling hiss as the port-side cable parted between a deck block and the capstan. It whipped back like an angry snake. Before I could blink, a roustabout and the prince had been cut down on the deck.

By the time we got down the two short flights of steps, the mate and a crowd of deckhands and passengers were already clustered around the sprawled figures.

"Oh, God! My leg! My leg!" the roustabout was crying in agony. His pants leg was ripped, and the odd angle of his right leg indicated a serious break. The prince was not moving or talking; he was unconscious.

"Musta slammed his head against the deck," Fin said as we worked our way to the fallen prince. His four companions were already there, but none of them appeared to be doing anything.

"Yeah," I agreed. "I don't see any marks on his head where the cable could've hit him. And he wasn't standing close enough to hit a stanchion or anything else."

As Fin knelt and began going over the prince, feeling cautiously for broken bones, I couldn't help but think that this was becoming a common sight—the young American sailor coming to the aid of the young Rumanian prince.

"Nothing seems to be broken. Grease down the side of his pants here where the cable whipped his legs out from under him. Good thing it didn't hit any higher." As he talked, he was checking the unconscious man's head. He stopped talking abruptly as his probing fingers came away from the back of his head, red and sticky. He felt again, carefully, and the prince moaned softly. "He's got a pretty good knot coming up back here, and he's got a small gash in his scalp, but unless he cracked his skull, I think he's all right." The prince groaned again and his eyes flickered open. He did not seem to know where he was. His eyes closed for a few seconds and then opened again. He lay there and focused on our faces, one at a time.

"Gentlemen," he finally said, his voice weak, "I've obviously had some sort of accident. If you would help me to my room, I'd be most grateful."

I turned to the mate for another litter similar to the canvas one they were sliding under the injured roustabout.

"No, no," Prince Zarahoff protested weakly. "Don't carry me. Just help me up. I can walk."

"Damnable pride!" Staghorn hissed, between his teeth. We raised him into a sitting position and held him there until the dizziness passed and he signaled for us to lift him. With his four men helping, we got him to his feet, trying to favor the gunshot gash across his left shoulder that had not had time to heal.

Just then Will Hosey reached the main deck. His eyes took in the situation immediately. "Velk!" he yelled at the mate. "How many times do I have to tell you to keep passengers away from the foredeck when this boat is grasshoppering?"

The mate swallowed and looked away, saying nothing.

157

"How bad are these men hurt?"

"He's got a knot on his head the size of a walnut and is bruised up some, but I don't think anything is broken," Fin replied as we eased the injured man up the steps, one at a time. "That deckhand took the worst of it."

"What about it, Velk?" Hosey demanded. "How bad is he?"

"Can't rightly say, Captain," the mate replied. "Leg's broke pretty bad, and maybe a rib, too. We'll have to get him to a hospital in Jefferson City."

"That is, if we get this boat off this damn bar before dark. Reeve that spare cable and let's get on with it,"

"It broke not too far from the end. I think we've still got enough to use."

"Get out the spare one, anyway. I don't want to take any chances. If that cable broke once, it's probably got other bad places in it and could break again."

I glanced back over my shoulder as we slowly ascended the steps and saw Hosey pick up the end of the loose cable and begin examining it. "Seems like your men could keep the gear in better shape."

The mate's face went red at these words. "Captain, as you can see, that cable was in perfect shape—no rust, no frays, and we've kept it well oiled. I know what kind of strain those things are under, and we don't take chances with them. In fact, the port cable was just replaced in Saint Louis about a week ago."

"Then, why in hell did it break?" Hosey asked sarcastically. Both men passed out of my sight as we reached the top of the steps to the boiler deck, and I couldn't catch the mate's reply.

No sooner had we got the prince into his cabin and onto the bed than a steward was there with alcohol, a

158

bottle of brandy, and some bandages. We slid his greasy trousers off and examined his legs. Purpling welts were forming on the backs and sides of both legs, and they were badly swollen, but there didn't appear to be any serious damage.

"A little of this brandy may ease the pain in my head," the prince said, pouring himself about a third of a glassful. "It seems fate continues to cause our paths to cross," he said, sipping the brandy and addressing me and Staghorn. He winced slightly as one of his men attempted to clean the matted blood from the hair on the back of his head. "I'm not sure that is a good sign. The last time we talked was aboard the *Silver Swan,* and I was being attended like this for a gunshot wound. I don't know if your country is just more hazardous than I expected, or if there is some intent behind all this."

"That's what we were trying to tell you before," Fin replied, a slight trace of irritation in his voice. "Although I don't know how this could have been anything but an accident."

"Ouch!" Prince Ferdinand jumped as Nicolae hurt his head. The prince turned angrily and spoke rapidly to him in Rumanian and then waved all four of them out of the room. They withdrew slowly into the adjoining cabin, all the while eyeing us suspiciously.

As soon as the door closed, the prince said in a lower voice, "I had to use some pretext to get them out of here so I could speak to you alone."

Our expressions showed our curiosity.

"This is difficult for me to say, but . . ." He paused and sipped the brandy, choosing his next words. "I am not one who admits mistakes easily. But I have been wrong."

"About what?" I asked, but thinking both of us

159

already knew what he was going to say.

"I have become convinced of the truth of your words to me earlier. I now believe that two and possibly all four of my men are trying to kill me."

"Surely you don't think they had anything to do with this accident?" I asked, wondering if the prince were not getting a little paranoid.

"Gentlemen, a piece of steel cable does not snap on command, unless it has been tampered with."

"Accidents happen all the time," Fin countered. "How could they have had anything to do with it?"

"Just before we began this—what do you call it?—grasshoppering maneuver, Nicolae suggested I might want to go down on deck to get a closer look. When we got down there, the mate tried to clear the deck, and we got into a fight."

"We saw it," Fin said.

"Nicolae was the one who urged me to stand where I was to get a good view. Then, after the mate pushed me, I would have stood where I was, regardless."

"So you think Nicolae was placing you so you'd be in a position to be injured or killed when that cable snapped, and that he had done something to it to make it snap?" Fin summed up.

"Yes. They retreated and left me standing there alone. They knew what would happen."

Staghorn and I looked our doubts at each other.

"I know you are not convinced, and I would not have thought anything about this either, except for something that happened last night."

"What?"

"Did you know that a steam line broke last night, just after supper?"

"Now that you mention it, I remember the engines

stopping and the boat going dead in the water for a time. I was doing some writing, and I didn't pay much attention. Just figured it was some mechanical problem."

"What happened?" Fin asked.

"Nicolae told me he had met a fellow Rumanian among the deck passengers, and thought I might be interested in meeting and talking with a man from our homeland. I thought it strange that I had been on this boat since leaving Saint Louis, and had not heard of this, but I went down with Nicolae to meet this man. I was curious. Alex was with us. As it happened, the man was actually from France. He had been born in Rumania, but his parents had taken him to France when he was a child. He knew almost nothing about our country. He could speak only a little of our language."

I couldn't imagine where this story was leading, but I leaned back against the wall and folded my arms, letting him go on in his unhurried way.

The prince paused and took a deep breath, sipped his brandy, and gingerly touched the back of his head with his other hand.

"We were standing near the port side talking under the overhang. It was by the little cross-passageway just in front of the enclosed deck area of the stern. The port-side steam line ran along just a foot or two over my head. Alex was leaning against a heavy beam that was propped up against some bales, apparently to make some repairs on one of the damaged braces. The beam turned under his weight, and its upper end fell against the steam line over my head. It knocked the steam line out of position and it ruptured at a seam. Alex jumped back when the beam gave way, but if it hadn't been for the Frenchman knocking me out of the way instantly, I

161

might have been scalded to death. As it was, the Frenchman's hand was burned, but not badly, when the live steam shot down out of the break in that pipe."

"And you don't think this was an accident?"

"No. Alex and Nicolae would surely know that this Frenchman was not Rumanian."

"Maybe you misunderstood what they said," Fin offered calmly. "It would be very unusual to run into anyone on this boat who was even born in your country."

"I did not misunderstand," Ferdinand Zarahoff declared, with some heat, and immediately winced as his head felt the effects. "No, I was lured down to the main deck on that pretext," he continued more calmly, but positively. "It was all just too convenient. I was told to wait in a certain place, and Alex brought the man to me to introduce him just where that spare beam was conveniently propped. And where that small passageway around cargo would allow the beam to fall against the steam line. No"—he shook his head slowly as if reluctant to give in to his suspicions—"there is just too much coincidence. You two were right all along. My retainers are out to kill me."

Staghorn and I looked at each other. Was the man asking for our help again? I, for one, did not want to get mixed up with him a second time. I was beginning to believe that Fin's superstitions were right—our royal visitor was bad luck. But then, what about my story? I had labored over it for several hours already. But, I reasoned, I could always finish it from the point of view of a spectator, rather than a participant. No, another part of me argued; the very essence and value of my feature story was its inside, intimate slant. I was glad when Fin finally broke the silence.

"Why don't you just send them packing?" he asked with blunt logic.

"I have considered that. But I think that maybe only Nicolae and Alex are involved. I feel that Ion and Karl are probably innocent. But I'm not sure."

"Have you discussed this with Ion and Karl?" I asked.

"No. If I'm wrong and they are in on this, too, then I've tipped them off that I am aware of their plot."

"Then send them all home," Fin repeated. "That way you'll be safe. You're the prince. Just tell them you've decided to finish this trip on your own. You can speak English and they can't. You don't need them to help you get along in this country. About all they do is wait on you or haul your luggage."

"The problem with that, my friends, is that I could never be sure they would go. I have no idea why they are trying to kill me. If they were hired by someone in my country, they would not dare go home without accomplishing their mission, or their own lives would be forfeit. So, if I put them off the boat at the next town that has a railroad, I would never feel safe the rest of this trip. I would be expecting a bullet in the back anywhere at any time. No," he said sadly, his thick mustache drooping, "I feel that my best chance is to have them close by where I can watch them."

"But they have opportunities every day—every hour—to kill you," I protested.

"Possibly," he nodded, "but they haven't succeeded so far. And the way they have gone about it, they apparently are not willing to sacrifice their own lives in some sort of suicidal attack. They always try to make it look like an accident."

"Except for that shooting episode in Saint Louis," Fin said.

163

"Yes, if it *was* Alex and Nicolae. However, they apparently want to eliminate me without implicating themselves. I have thought about trying to write my father to see if he can enlighten me about this, but his reply would never catch up with me. I plan to stay only for the summer, and it is already early July. I must meet your famous scout, Buffalo Bill Cody at Bismarck on July fifteenth."

"There will be all kinds of opportunities to shoot you on a buffalo hunt and make it look like an accident," I observed.

The prince glanced up sharply. "One way or another, I plan to be rid of these four before then."

Fin and I glanced at each other. "You don't plan to kill them?" I asked finally. I had heard that a traditional way of dealing with potential assassins in eastern European countries was to kill them before they could kill you, proof of guilt be damned.

"Only in self-defense," he replied, and I let out a small sigh of relief. The prospect of a distinguished foreign visitor being tried for murder in the American courts was not a pleasant one.

"My father hired these men, and I had thought of trying to forge a letter from him recalling them to Rumania. But I could never duplicate his writing or the royal seal."

"Put it in the form of a telegram," Staghorn suggested.

"Father would never operate that way, and these men know it. He would have a handwritten message delivered by a courier. He loves to use the trappings of the monarchy."

"Do you have any idea at all who would benefit from your death?" I asked.

"If my retainers are acting on their own, all they could possibly gain would be the personal possessions I have brought along—nothing of any great value. A few jewels, some money, a couple of finely crafted English guns, and my clothing. Taken together, worth a total of possibly five thousand pounds. If they could turn it all into American dollars, no more than twenty thousand— not a great sum when split among four men, or even two, considering the risks they are exposing themselves to."

Fin and I nodded in agreement. Apparently, Prince Ferdinand Zarahoff was not as naive as he at first appeared. He had thought this whole matter through very carefully.

"If, on the other hand," he continued in his pleasant, slightly British accent, "they were hired by someone else, their rewards could be considerably greater. There are many pretenders to the throne in my country, many with political ambitions. And since I am the heir. . ." He shrugged, leaving the obvious conclusion hanging in the air.

"What do you want us to do, Prince Ferdinand?" Fin finally asked in a tone that a royal subject might use. Gone were all misunderstandings, hurt pride, and self-interests that had marred their earlier relationship. Here was a fellow human who was in trouble, with no one else for thousands of miles to turn to. The man's station in life was far different from our own, but it was obvious that social status and wealth did not guarantee immunity from trouble.

"Nothing for the moment," he replied slowly. "Just watch me and my men very closely. I would take much comfort in the fact that you are ready and willing to come to my aid in any emergency."

165

"We can't watch you at night," Fin objected. "Even when we were sleeping in your room, they got away from us."

"That was my own fault for going ashore alone," the prince replied. "I don't believe they would do anything so foolish as knifing me in my sleep. And I have been very careful about what I eat and drink. From now on I will be most cautious about where I venture and with whom I talk on this boat." He gestured at the noise that had begun again as the grasshoppering resumed. "Barring too many more groundings or accidents, I should be on this boat at least another ten or twelve days. I hope by then that my various wounds and bruises will be healed sufficiently to allow me to ride without difficulty. If you can hold them off, somehow, for the next fortnight until I meet the hunting party, I will make it well worth your while." He looked at us expectantly.

I noticed the sag of his shoulders and the pain in his brown eyes, and I began to see the real Ferdinand Zarahoff, not as a member of European royalty, but as a vulnerable and injured young man, inexperienced in the ways of the world, alone in a strange country and much in need of help and someone to trust. The irritating air of command he used as a shield was down, and I saw him again as I had seen him once before—on the night we had shared a drink after our dunking in the river.

Fin waved a hand deprecatingly. "We don't want your money. If an American can't help someone in trouble without hope of reward, he isn't worth much, in my opinion."

I nodded my agreement.

"Thank you, gentlemen." He smiled for the first time. "But we'll talk about that when the time comes. Right now, I'll bid you good day, or my men will begin to suspect something, if they haven't already." He reached out and gripped the right hand of each of us in turn, and the barriers of royalty dissolved.

"Bad as it is sometimes, with corruption and political scandals, I'll still take our form of government over his any day," I remarked as we emerged onto the open end of the boiler deck a couple of minutes later.

"I'll go along with that one hundred percent," Staghorn agreed.

CHAPTER 16

"Oh, whiskey killed my sister Sue,
And whiskey killed the old man, too,
Whiskey for my Johnny!"

"CAN'T YOU SING A MORE CHEERFUL SONG?" I complained. "Or one with a little more tune to it? Some of those chanteys at least have a good melody."

"Yeah, but this one's got several hundred verses to it, and I could probably think up some more," Fin grinned at me. But he dropped the singsong chantey and left us with nothing but the belching noise of escaping steam and the vibrations of machinery as the *Yankton* churned smoothly upriver beyond Omaha eight days later. The Fourth of July had come and gone, and our small contingent of passengers and crew had observed it at the Herndon House Hotel in Omaha with speeches by local politicians and a fireworks display. Everyone on the *Yankton* had been treated to a free beef dinner and beer on board. The immigrant deck passengers were

167

included, but some of them had only the vaguest idea of what the celebration was all about. Most of the roustabouts who were not on duty went ashore and came back early the next morning in various stages of repair and sobriety.

But Independence Day was behind us and nearly forgotten now as Fin and I sat in our wooden deck chairs outside our rooms and watched the green of the slowly changing riverbank slide by. We were unobtrusively watching the prince, who sat about forty feet away, his feet propped on the rail, reading a magazine. The four Rumanians were nowhere in sight. Things had been quiet, almost monotonous, during the past few days. I doubted that our careful vigilance had anything to do with it, but no further attempts had been made on the prince's life. His injuries were healing nicely in the meantime. Will Hosey had confirmed that the broken cable had been sawed or filed most of the way through. But discovering who had done it or why remained impossible.

"You already beginning to miss the ocean?" I inquired, glancing sideways at Fin.

"Yeah," he admitted. "Not shipboard life, but the ocean. The sea gets a grip on a man. I don't know what there is about it."

"Maybe part of your English and Scandinavian heritage coming out in you," I suggested.

"Maybe," he agreed, looking hungrily out over the cottonwoods and smaller trees at the countryside, beyond. It was more and more open prairie with only patches of woods, like small islands.

"I think it'll have to be prairie farming or the sea for you," I continued. "You'll never be happy working in an office or store, or grubbing for a living on a little pig and tobacco farm back in the hills. You were born for the wide-open spaces."

"I'd like to get a little more schooling before I tackle anything for good," he replied. "It looks like the big operators have taken over the prairie farming already, from what Captain Hosey was telling us yesterday."

"Yes. But how many operations are there like that of the Grandin brothers? They may have thousands of acres in the Red River Valley producing record wheat yields, but that doesn't mean there isn't plenty of room for the small farmer, too. The Grandins have to depend on the weather just like the settlers who live in sod houses or dugouts. And think of the overhead they must have with the harvesters, the livestock, the hired help, the grain storage. Besides, Hosey said they had some government funds to help them get started. And how long do you think that soil will stay fertile if they plant the same crop every year without fertilizer?"

"Don't know. I'm no farmer. At least not yet. Maybe never will be," he added. He shrugged. As he looked toward me I noticed that his badly bruised face had nearly healed up. And he looked as if he had gained a good five to ten pounds since I had first met him. His gaunt cheeks had filled out somewhat so that his face was flat, smooth planes, and his whip-thin body looked more compact. In spite of the hazards and strain he had been under since the beginning of this river voyage, the good food and sleep had done wonders for him. His last voyage around the Horn before coming ashore must indeed have been a hard one. We sat quietly, without speaking, for a few minutes, drinking in the freshness of the summer morning. Fin pulled out his harmonica, wiped it off and softly began to play "Old Folks at Home."

"You know," I remarked, my thoughts drifting back to the prince, who sat a few yards down the deck from us, "even though nothing has happened since that cable snapped over a week ago, I keep feeling a tension in the air—like something else is about to happen."

"It may be your imagination," Fin replied in a low voice. "Knowing that we're guarding him again." He shrugged and wiped his harmonica on his sleeve. "I don't notice anything different. They may just be lying low, waiting for another good opportunity."

"Well, it's frustrating knowing who your enemies are, but not being able to confront them. Just have to wait around for them to make the first move before we can react."

"I know. I'd have thrown them off the boat long ago. I guess the Eastern mind is a little more devious than ours."

"But the closer we get to Bismarck, the more nervous I get," I said.

"We're a long way from Bismarck yet. In fact, with all the delays we've had, the, prince is never going to meet his hunting party by July fifteenth."

"He sent a wire to Buffalo Bill Cody from Omaha. When it's your party, you don't have to worry about anyone starting without you." I grinned.

"I guess not. But you don't want to start across Dakota and Montana too late in the season, either."

"By the way, you said you were going to visit your folks. Where do they live?"

"They're homesteading on a little farm fifty to sixty miles northeast of Yankton."

"If you go all the way to Bismarck, you'll have to backtrack a long way, then."

"Yes, but I'm in no big hurry. I wrote them from New

170

Orleans telling them I'd be home in time to help with harvest, but didn't give them any definite date. It'll be good to see the folks and my sisters again, but swinging a cradle in a wheat field doesn't sound as exciting as meeting Buffalo Bill. I'm looking forward to seeing some of that upper Missouri country, too. Never been there before."

"I hear there's not much different about it. It's all about as flat as this deck, according to the captain."

"That's my kind of country," Fin replied with a smile. "I'm a flat-lander, born and reared. Maybe that's the reason I took to the sea so easily."

"I've gotten used to the wide-open spaces in the past year or so, but I still like the security of trees around me. I feel exposed on the plains, like a big bug that could get stepped on."

"I think I know what you mean," he replied thoughtfully. "It's a feeling of being insignificant in the vastness of the land and sky. It's a vulnerable feeling like I had when I experienced my first storm at sea."

Our conversation drifted on to other subjects during the next hour or so as we whiled away the pleasant morning. I finally suggested going up to the pilothouse to see if Captain Will Hosey was on duty, but Fin reminded me of our promise not to let Prince Ferdinand Zarahoff out of our sight, except at night.

"You're right," I replied. "Besides, we don't want to wear out our welcome in the wheelhouse."

"At least we weren't up there when he went aground three times this week."

"Right. We can't be blamed for that. But one of those groundings was done by Wiggins, the other pilot."

"I still admire these men who can damn near float these wedding cakes on a heavy dew."

171

"Probably why they can't afford to insure them for more than a fraction of their value. Too many hazards."

Our conversation dropped as the call came for dinner, and we went inside to a hearty lunch of beef and potatoes and fried corn. We were even served some fresh, boiled turnip greens picked up at the last stop.

"I know I won't want any supper, after all this," I said. "Not enough exercise to work it off."

"Yeah. I'm really looking forward to going ashore this afternoon when we wood up near Sioux City."

"I'd forgotten about that. Hosey said we could even walk on into town and the boat would meet us there about suppertime."

"Sounds good to me; I need to stretch my legs," Fin said, a little too loudly, I thought. "I wonder who-all is going ashore?" I glanced at Fin, and he was looking directly across the white linen tablecloth at the prince, who appeared to be paying no attention. I was beginning to wonder if the prince had even heard Fin's comment over the hum of voices and the clanking of silverware. But just then the prince tipped up his water glass and gave Fin a barely perceptible look of acknowledgment.

It was less than an hour after lunch when we approached the woodyard about a mile below Sioux City. No sooner were the mooring lines heaved across and the landing stage lowered, than the deck passengers and cabin passengers began streaming ashore. Fin and I were in the vanguard. The Army Corps of Engineers officers and their sunbonneted wives, the ragged Irish immigrants with their barefooted children, even the buckskin-clad frontiersman scattered out singly and in small groups and began climbing the rounded hills. I looked back as we were

172

halfway up and put out my hand to stop Staghorn.

"Where's the prince?"

As the last stragglers came off the gangway, Prince Zarahoff appeared in knee-high boots, light shirt, and straw hat. His four retainers were in his wake. One of them was carrying a picnic basket.

Fin and I trudged on up the steepening hill, knowing the prince was in view. The exercise felt good after our many days of nothing more strenuous than strolling a deck and occasionally climbing a short flight of stairs. We finally reached the summit, slightly out of breath, and turned to view the scene behind us. The *Yankton* had shrunk to the size of a large toy where it lay it the bank, gray smoke from its tall chimneys drifting northward on the breeze. The woodyard was a fairly level space on the shore, backed and nearly surrounded by a copse of trees. Two great cottonwoods dominated the yard, and the gnarled, hundred-foot giants also provided plenty of shade. With only the woods that lined the water and a few scattered groves back from the river, I couldn't imagine where the woodhawks found enough timber to provide a regular service to the steamboats. But from where we stood, I could see several cords stacked back under the trees. I suspected that much of it was probably cottonwood, elm, and such driftwood as they could salvage, rather than the good hardwood we had gotten downstream. The roustabouts were moving steadily back and forth on their usual daily chore of loading and stacking the wood on deck for the voracious fireboxes that consumed two dozen cords of wood every twenty-four running hours.

I lifted my hat and wiped a sleeve across my damp forehead. "This breeze sure feels good."

"Yeah. I've missed this prairie wind. Hot and dry as it

gets, it sure beats the sultry heat along the Gulf Coast," Staghorn replied.

We walked along the top of the hill, stretching and breathing deeply of the fresh air. The early afternoon sun was bearing down fiercely, burning through the back of my shirt, but the breeze dried the perspiration from our bodies so quickly that I was reasonably cool and comfortable. I glanced to my right and saw a group of women deck passengers who had discovered a thicket of wild blackberries. They were talking excitedly as they picked and ate the ripe fruit. Some of them were putting the berries in wicker baskets.

Other groups of passengers were strolling about, much as we were doing. Some of the immigrant children were having a contest to see which of them could throw a rock far enough to reach the river from where they stood near the summit of the hill. From the number of people ashore, it appeared nobody but the roustabouts, could be left aboard. I mentioned as much to Staghorn.

"I was talking to a drummer yesterday," Fin replied. "He makes this run up to Fort Benton regularly, and he told me that on up where the timber really thins out, all the passengers have to go ashore regularly, not just for exercise, and relaxation, but to scour up enough fallen timber and driftwood to get the boat to the next woodyard."

"I'm glad the roustabouts are still the only ones who have to take care of that. Let's hope there'll be enough wood between here and Bismarck."

Captain Hosey lifted his hand in greeting as he strode up the hill toward us. "If you gents are walking into town, I'll join you," Hosey called as soon as he was within hailing distance. He came up to us through the

174

lush grass, slightly winded, and the three of us strolled on toward the settlement of Sioux City the better part of a mile away.

"We'll take on some stores here," the pilot was saying. "Yankton is now the real terminus of the railroad, and most of the freight and military supplies go from there. But now and again we can arrange for a good load here at Sioux City. We'll drop some cargo and a few passengers and cram all the cargo aboard that we have room for groceries, furniture, medicine, whiskey, and a lot of other stuff they need at those upper Missouri forts. We underbid the Coulson Line this year for the contract to haul military supplies. We'll use every inch of space we have. Probably take us a day or so to load. You'll play hell getting around the decks between here and Bismarck with all the cargo that'll be lashed down and stuck in every nook and cranny." He grinned. "Aside from goin' ashore, the only exercise you'll get from now on is gettin' up and down from the table and getting in and out of bed.

"Navigatin' will be pure hell, loaded down thataway; she'll be drawin' over four and a half feet. But even if we have to do some off-loadin' or some double-trippin', the profits will be worth it. We have to get as much as we can for every trip. The railroad is going to be touchin' those upper ports like Running Water, Chamberlain and Pierre in the next couple o' years, and then it'll be all over for the steamers, except for pickin' up the crumbs. The Northern Pacific already has a line into Bismarck from the east."

Even though I was a relative latecomer to steamboat travel, I felt a slight twinge of nostalgia at his words, and some pity for the man himself. He would no doubt finish his days at the wheel of a riverboat, no matter how much the packet trade might change or decline in the coming years. But Hosey seemed to take it as a realistic matter of course. If he had any regrets, his voice didn't betray them.

We walked down the slope on the far side of the hill, out of sight of the landing. We passed under a large cottonwood tree whose shade provided blessed relief from the burning sun. A meadowlark trilled in the distance. Two redwinged blackbirds flashed up from the direction of the willows along the river that was out of sight to our left.

A short blast on a steam whistle came to our ears.

"Ah, they're finished wooding up. Wiggins'll be backin' her out and takin 'er down to the landing in town. We'll join 'er there." Hosey smiled at us and pushed his hat back on his head. "Believe it or not, it's just as nice for me to get a break from that boat as it is for you. Everybody appreciates a day off from work now and again—even if he enjoys his job. I wonder what the cook's whippin' up for supper?"

At his remark, my mind drifted off onto the thought of food, as if I hadn't eaten all day. My appetite had returned with a vengeance.

WWHHOOOOOOMMM!!

The concussion of the explosion was louder than a whole battery of artillery. My heart jumped into my throat. I knew instinctively what it was, but I blocked out the thought. Hosey recovered his presence of mind first and went dashing back up the hill toward the sound. Fin and I were right behind him. In the few seconds it took us to race out from under the shelter of the cottonwood, a hundred thoughts flashed through my mind. But then the source of the blast burst on my vision and my throat closed up in horror. A cloud of

176

steam and smoke was mushrooming up from the woodyard and the air around me was suddenly filled with falling objects—wood, shards of glass, shredded bits of metal. I hit the ground and covered my head against the falling debris. The boat's brass bell hit the slope near me and went rolling and clanging down the hill toward the river. Bits and pieces of flaming wood fell, hissing, into the water. Through a thick pall of smoke and steam I could see the flaming hulk of what had been the *Yankton* drifting slowly out from the bank into midstream. Only the back half of the superstructure remained, and it was leaning askew, part of its already beginning to burn. As the last bits of burning wreckage landed and set fire to the dry grass here and there, a few seconds of ghastly silence fell over the shattered scene. Except for the drifting smoke and leaping flames from the hull, the picture before me seemed frozen and unchanging. Then screams of agony and fear rose on all sides. I was almost in shock myself and was hardly aware that I had stood up and was watching Hosey and Staghorn running with several of the other passengers who had been ashore. In addition to the wreckage that littered the hillside and the surface of the river, there was also grisly evidence of the human toll—bloody pieces of arms and legs, smoldering clothing, portions of trunks, and even a blackened head. Scalded but living victims who had been blown into the water by the explosion were grasping at floating wreckage and crying pitifully for help. As the reality of the disaster struck me, I struggled to quell the nausea that rose in my stomach and ran to do what I could to help the survivors.

CHAPTER 17

IT HAD BEEN TWO DAYS SINCE THE *YANKTON* HAD blown herself to kindling at the Sioux City woodyard. Wiggins, the pilot, had been instantly killed, along with the first engineer, ten roustabouts, four deck passengers and one cabin passenger—a drummer who was asleep in his room. In addition to the sixteen killed outright, seven others were blown into the water and suffered burns and contusions. Two of these were badly scalded and not expected to live. Two others were missing and presumed dead. Fin and I had assisted the other passengers and crew who were ashore in rescuing the survivors and rushing them to medical assistance in the town.

"I just don't know," Will Hosey was saying that night after supper as he twirled his third whiskey in his hands at the hotel bar. Several of us sat at the bar trying to console him for his loss. "Boiler explosions like that were pretty common when I first went on the river," the pilot lamented, staring into his glass. "But it's pretty rare of late. About the only cases I've heard of in the last two years were the result of some fool hard-firing his boilers with pine knots or resin and oil, and maybe tying down the safety valve, or trying to keep up steam for a fast getaway from a landing. I just can't figure out what happened. And Fred was a good engineer. He didn't take chances. He wouldn't have let the water level get low or unbalanced. Maybe we had a faulty gauge."

"Aren't there a lot of different things that could have caused it?" Fin asked.

"Oh, sure. Excessive wear and corrosion of boilers, a bad rivet, a defective supply pump, a clogged connecting

178

pipe, an accumulation of mud in the boilers. But we were careful to keep our machinery in top shape."

We did what we could to console, him, but he felt worst about the loss of life, which he considered his responsibility. The monetary loss of his boat and cargo and the blot on his reputation as a pilot and owner were only secondary in his mind after the human calamity.

Fin and I had taken a room in one of the better hotels of Sioux City, along with Hosey and the prince and his men and most of the cabin passengers. Staghorn and I had privately discussed the possibility that the boiler explosion might have been purposely caused, but after turning the matter over and examining, it from all angles we came to the conclusion that it was most unlikely. Before supper, we managed to get the prince alone in the lobby and confided our views to him. He agreed that, even though it might have been possible for one of his men to jam the steam gauge, or tie down the safety valve, or block the water intake and maybe fool an inattentive engineer, the odds that this had happened were very long indeed. If one of the prince's men had managed to sabotage the machinery to cause this disaster, they surely would have seen to it that the prince himself had stayed aboard. But the prince assured us that none of his men had even suggested he stay on the boat that afternoon.

The townspeople of Sioux City had turned out in force to make the survivors welcome in their town, to care for the injured, and to arrange for burying the dead. They donated food and clothing to many of the deck passengers who had been left completely destitute. The storekeepers gave credit to total strangers. Charity bolstered all the survivors until they could get their lives back on track again.

"Yankton! Yankton!" the conductor shouted in a singsong voice as he hauled himself up the aisle of the coach, grabbing the back of every other seat as if walking uphill.

I jerked myself fully awake and looked out the soot-streaked glass beside me. I rubbed my red eyes and looked again as the train slowed. This town at the junction of the James and Missouri Rivers wasn't at all what I had expected. Instead of the ramshackle community of rough log and mud dwellings and tents I was prepared for, this was a town of substantial proportions. It had the look of settled permanence. There were some wooden buildings, but most of the structures in the business district appeared to be of brick, many of them two-storey.

"This place sure doesn't look like the mudhole I remember on my trip downriver six years ago," Staghorn said over my shoulder. "I doubt if the place had over seven hundred people in it then, counting hogs and chickens. Guess it got built up before it lost out to Bismarck as the territorial capital."

Prince Zarahoff was in the seat ahead of us and his retainers just beyond him. They, too, stared out the windows, but were silent.

Fin and I each had a small leather grip with a few spare clothes we had bought in Sioux City. I had come ashore with about $50 in my pocket, and Staghorn habitually carried his entire savings of about $200 in greenbacks in his pants pocket. I had cautioned him about carrying cash on his person, but he had shrugged off my urgings that he deposit it in the boat's safe. "That's all I had left after I bought my passage on this packet. Not much to show after six years of hard work,

180

is it?" he remarked to me as we paid for our meager purchases in a Sioux City dry goods store.

"I guess you were right after all to keep that money on you," I answered as we each rolled up one set of underwear, one pair of socks, a shirt, and a pair of Levi Strauss spring-bottom overall pants and stuffed them into our new leather bags. "Luckily, most of my savings is in a Chicago bank, safe and sound. But there are two things I did lose that really hurt."

"What's that?"

"My Winchester and my writing case with all of my story about Prince Zarahoff."

"But you can replace those."

"You're right. It'll be a lot of work, but I can reconstruct my story. That rifle and I have been through a lot together. But it was mighty heavy to carry around. I may buy a lighter carbine later. I was carrying my father's gold Waltham pocket watch. Nothing could have replaced the sentimental value attached to that if I had lost it."

Since we had lost nearly everything but the clothes on our backs, the prince, had insisted on paying for our railroad tickets on the Dakota Southern connecting line to Yankton, about seventy miles away. So here we were, the third day after the explosion, pulling into the Yankton depot about half past six. The sun was slanting long shadows across the dusty streets as the train finally ground to a halt at the station platform.

I grabbed my bag and started for the door, hardly able to wait to get some fresh air. We had kept the windows closed the entire trip to keep out the heat and dust and fine cinders.

"Looks like this place tried to become an important town and didn't quite make it," I commented as we gathered on the station platform with Prince Zarahoff and his men.

"It'll never be another Omaha," Fin replied, glancing along the nearly deserted street that trailed on out onto the flat prairie about three blocks away. "Even the railroad doesn't go any farther."

The normal prairie wind had subsided with the coming of sundown, and the dusty heat was oppressive. The only sound was the panting and steaming of the engine and the shuffling of feet on the wooden platform as other passengers debarked.

"Hack, gentlemen?" A lean, stoop-shouldered man with a tobacco-stained mustache lounged forward from the side of the depot. "Got four nice hotels in town if you gents are looking for a place to stay." He indicated a one-horse wagon with a canvas top. Its canvas sides had been rolled up and tied out of the way.

"Yes," the prince replied immediately. "Take us to the best hotel you have."

"You got any luggage?" the driver inquired, glancing around.

"This is it," Staghorn answered, holding up his small valise.

The seven of us climbed up into the hack and the driver untied the horse, took his seat, clucked softly to the animal, and turned into the main street.

I sat in the rear of the two bench seats in the hack and watched the tall, lanky Ion in front of me slapping the dust from his clothing, although he didn't seem any dustier than anyone else. Before we reached the hotel, two blocks away, he had taken out a small penknife and was carefully cleaning his fingernails.

Only since we had begun secretly guarding the prince again had I begun to take note of his four men individually. Since they rarely spoke, and then only to each other in their native tongue, it was hard to relate to them in any way. The four of them seemed to run together, like one, big, dark cloud that was constantly hovering nearby.

I was still studying Ion when we debarked in front of our two-storey brick hotel. He had a smooth shave, and his thick mustache was neatly trimmed, in contrast to Nicolae and Alex, who had not shaved since most of their belongings and razors were lost on the *Yankton*. Karl wore a full beard, but still looked somewhat unkempt and disheveled. The tall, sad-eyed Ion had evidently visited the hotel barber sometime that morning before we left Sioux City.

But the fact that he was neat in his personal appearance did nothing to help us determine his real attitude toward the prince, I reflected as our royal visitor paid the driver and we went into the lobby to register.

"Will you be taking the next steamer north for Bismarck?" Fin asked the prince as the six of us sat at supper in the hotel dining room. He spoke rather carefully, glancing sidelong at the four Rumanians on his left. Even though the prince had told us that they understood only a tiny bit of English and spoke it not at all, we were both very circumspect around them. Most of the time they either ignored us completely or watched us with hard, suspicious eyes, and I was constantly uncomfortable in their presence, not knowing how much, if any, of my talk they might understand.

"I will not be continuing my trip by steamboat," the young prince replied, selecting a thigh from the platter of fried chicken in front of us. "I've quite had my fill of river travel for now. I've been toying with the idea of

183

outfitting us with mounts and going the rest of the way on horseback."

My heart sank at this, remembering how saddle-weary and weather-beaten I had gotten the previous summer while on campaign with General Buck's Third Cavalry.

"But I have thought better of that," he went on, "for several reasons. First of all, I feel that I might need a scout who is familiar with the country, even though I could follow the river and eventually find my way to Bismarck. And I'm sure that Buffalo Bill Cody will have selected a mount for me that will be perfectly suited to the terrain and the type of hunting we will be doing. And lastly, I'm not sure I want to test myself physically on so strenuous a trip just before my hunting expedition."

"Speaking of your physical condition," Fin said around a mouthful of fresh bread, "how are you feeling?"

"I'm healing up marvelously," the prince replied, wiping his mouth on his napkin and grinning hugely under his dark mustache. "My shoulder is still a little sore, but the wound is sifting in where the flesh was gouged away. My legs and buttocks are still somewhat discolored, but I'm nearly as strong as before."

"How are you planning to get to Bismarck, then?" I asked. "This is already the tenth of July. You have only five days to meet your hunting party."

The prince was all business in a moment. "Before leaving Sioux City, I found out that there is a stagecoach line that connects these river towns. We will take passage on a coach. This should put us in Bismarck just in time, without taxing my physical stamina too greatly."

"Huh! You've apparently never ridden any distance in a stagecoach," I remarked. Prince Zarahoff's head jerked up sharply, but he relaxed when he saw I was smiling at him.

"I can't imagine it being any more hazardous, or any more boring, than steamboating on your western rivers," he added, signaling a white-aproned waitress for a piece of apple pie.

I wondered about the prince's finances. Had his supply of gold coins gone into the river with the boat's safe? Had he drawn a draft on some distant account through a bank in Sioux City? Or did he carry in his pockets what would be a small fortune to most normal men? I could not even fathom a guess, since my previous experience with royalty was nil. And I did not presume to question him about it, especially in front of his four men.

I leaned back in my chair, my stomach full, and sipped at a glass of water, enjoying the knowledge that my connection with Prince Zarahoff would soon be coming to an end. In no more than five days we would be in Bismarck, and our job as bodyguards would end.

Our meal was finished a few minutes later. The prince spoke briefly to his men in Rumanian, and they withdrew toward the stairs. Ferdinand Zarahoff, Fin Staghorn, and I walked out into the gathering dusk in a vain search for a cool breeze. The temperature was dropping slightly with the coming of darkness, but I estimated that it was still at least ninety degrees.

Yankton seemed to have an ample supply of saloons in proportion to its size. In fact, as we walked around the town, it appeared that about a third of its buildings were saloons, or saloons and restaurants combined.

We finally gave up trying to cool off and turned into a

large saloon and found a table near the door. Fin and I ordered beer, and the prince got a whiskey and water.

"I told my men I was going with you to get a drink, and that they were free to go wherever they wished," the prince said, sipping tentatively at his whiskey.

"They looked like school kids who were being scolded," Fin laughed.

"Ah, don't be deceived," the prince said gravely. "They are all very intelligent—and very deadly—men." He shook his head slowly. "I have given this matter much thought. I have combed my memory for details of their behavior since my father first engaged them to accompany me on this journey. Maybe it is only the suspicions gained by hindsight, but I feel very strongly that there were several instances of things one or the other of them said or did—little things, mind you—that were of no significance at the time, but which, in light of later developments, indicate to me that they were, even then, planning to do me harm. I cannot give you any examples of this, because they were only little, subtle things." He waved his hand in exasperation, then dug out a handkerchief and wiped his clammy brow. The air in the room was close and unmoving.

We sipped our drinks in silence for a few minutes, each of us with his own thoughts.

"Gentlemen," the prince finally said, looking up at us, "I have a strong feeling that another, and possibly final, attempt will be made on my life between now and the time we reach Bismarck. I have no concrete reason for believing this; it is only a feeling. They will not wait until I am engaged on my buffalo hunt to make another attempt on my life."

"Why?" Fin asked. "It would sure be a lot easier to arrange an accident in a crowd of people during the

186

excitement of a hunt in a remote area."

"I am tired of this cat-and-mouse game," the prince replied grimly. "So I plan to force their hand *if*, in fact, they are guilty of conspiracy and attempted assassination. I told them last night that I plan to dismiss them and send them home as soon as we reach Bismarck."

"Did they ask why?"

"They are my servants, and I am a prince. They do not question my orders or my wishes."

It was a sharp reminder that democracy did not rule everywhere.

A few minutes later Fin asked, "Prince Zarahoff, do you have any idea at all why these men would want you dead?"

"We've discussed this before, gentlemen. I have none. I wish to God I did! If I dismiss these men now, they may be waiting for me when I get home, and I do not wish to be watching my back for weeks or months to come. I am giving them one last chance to show their hand, as you American poker players say. If they do nothing, I will have to assume they are innocent and that someone else is trying to kill me." He raised his glass. "To the defeat of one's enemies!"

"Here's to a swift and safe trip to Bismarck," I countered.

He tossed off his whiskey, neat, and chased it with a swallow of water. He made a wry face. "It will take much longer than I have on this trip to become accustomed to American frontier whiskey *and* frontier water."

CHAPTER 18

THE NEXT DAY DAWNED HOT AND CLOUDLESS. BY THE time we had eaten a substantial breakfast in the hotel dining room and assembled at the stage station a block away the temperature was already well into the eighties. The prevailing south wind was picking up dust from the hooves of horses and passing wagon wheels in the street and swirling it into the eyes of our party standing on the boardwalk.

I was wearing the white, collarless cotton shirt I had bought in Sioux City and the new Levi pants that flared out near the bottom to accommodate boots. Since the pants had only a drawstring lace in the back, and no belt loops, I wore suspenders. A low-crowned straw hat completed the outfit. Fin's attire was very similar, except that he wore no gun. The prince and all four of his men were carrying .45s in new-looking holsters and gun belts. If these were newly purchased weapons for their American trip, I wondered how well any of them could shoot. But then I remembered the wounding of the prince in a dark alley back in Saint Louis, while Fin and I had hit nothing. But then, anyone could get off a lucky shot in the dark. If they had had a clear shot from ambush, the prince should really be dead, instead of nursing a groove along, the top of his shoulder muscle.

"Look, mister, we've got other passengers going out on this stage," the voice of the ticket agent came to me through the open doorway of the stage office. I looked in to see Prince Zarahoff talking to a heavyset, balding man who had come out from behind the counter and was confronting the young prince. "These three gents

188

are going up to Pierre, and they've had their tickets for the better part of a week—bought and paid for."

"Our party of seven is going through to Bismarck," Prince Ferdinand replied evenly and logically. "I wish to reserve a coach for our own use, at least as far as Pierre, to avoid being too crowded in this heat. It is a long trip," he added, in his most soothing voice.

But the ticket agent was not listening. His round face was growing increasingly red above the stiff collar. "We've put as many as fifteen people aboard one of our coaches, plus luggage, when need be," the agent said. "Several of 'em ride up top. These three men"—he swept a beefy hand at the three standing nearby watching this exchange—"have business in Pierre. They are some of this town's leading citizens. Besides, this is a public stage line. Anyone can buy a ticket if we have room." He turned his back on the prince and returned to his place behind the counter. "And we do have room," he said with finality, picking up a piece of chalk to mark the arrival time of the next stage on a wall blackboard behind him.

The prince reached into his pocket and produced a small buckskin poke. He pulled the drawstring open and poured several gold coins onto the counter. That pretty well answered my earlier question about the state of his finances. At the sound of the jingle, the agent turned back around. He eyed the gleaming pile and then looked blankly at the prince.

"I am reserving this coach," Prince Ferdinand repeated, persistently, as if he had not heard anything the agent said.

"Look, Mr. . . . whatever your name is. You talk like some kind of foreigner, so maybe you don't know how things are done here. This is not your private coach.

189

There are others here who had their tickets before you and your friends did."

"I am prepared to buy these other gentlemen's tickets, and to offer them a handsome profit." He glanced at the three waiting passengers and smiled briefly. "I'm sure they won't mind waiting for the next stage."

"Dammit, I said you can't do it!" the agent exploded, reddening again. "Who the hell do you think you are, the King of Siam?"

"I am Prince Ferdinand Zarahoff, of Rumania, on an official visit to this country," the prince announced, in his most imperious tone, drawing himself up to his full height. "And I wish for me and my companions to have some degree of comfort on the last portion of our trip to Bismarck to meet your famous scout, Buffalo Bill Cody."

The agent hesitated, looking from the pile of gold coins to the prince's face and then glancing uncertainly at the rest of us, who had edged inside the doorway. He looked suddenly unsure of himself, as if he couldn't decide whether or not he was being slickered. But there was no denying the reality of the gold on the counter.

"If you gentlemen will accept this offer," the prince said, turning to the three waiting passengers, "I will make it worth your while."

The three glanced inquiringly at each other. Finally, one of them shrugged and stepped forward. "Well, I don't reckon I have anything so important that it can't wait a day or so. A prince's money is as good as anyone's." He smiled and held out his ticket.

The other two quickly followed his lead, sold their tickets at a healthy profit, and departed, apparently pleased with their deal. The agent, seeing that he was no longer in control of the situation, busied himself shuffling papers and pretended to ignore us.

"Let's get aboard, folks. We're moving out on time." A broad-shouldered man with a sweeping mustache and a hat pushed back on his head stood in the open doorway.

We filed out and climbed into the big Concord coach.

"This is going to be dusty as the devil, but at least we won't suffocate from the heat," I observed to Fin as I sat in the back of the coach and indicated the canvas window flaps rolled up and tied.

He nodded his assent. "Don't know how this thing could've held fifteen without being jammed on top of each other." He flung a small cotton sack of belongings under the seat.

Nicolae sat next to me; the muscular Alex with his handlebar mustache on our far right, the three of us facing forward. Riding backward and facing us were Fin, the prince, and the quiet, bearded Karl, while Ion, at the driver's invitation, sat up above with him. The middle seat was vacant, and we used it to rest our legs on. Our valises were in the rear boot, with the exception of the flat leather case Karl carried. I didn't know what it contained. Could be that the prince didn't want to entrust his currency or gold to the luggage boot.

The driver popped his whip, and the four horses lunged into the traces as the coach pulled away. We passed a few men on horseback and several men and women on the sidewalk. A buckboard and a farm wagon stood at the hitching rail of a general store. A solid-looking brick bank passed quickly, then another block of stores, saloons, and restaurants spun past. The buildings began to thin out quickly as the horses' ground-eating trot put Yankton behind us. Suddenly we were on the vast Dakota prairie, heading generally

191

northwest along a road that was only a double-track trail across the undulating land whose grass was burned dun-colored by the merciless sun. The driver let out the horses, and the deep-chested sorrels eagerly stretched into a run, burning off their early energy. I was sure our driver wouldn't let them go at this pace long after we got out of sight of town.

I glanced out through the dust cloud being churned up from the dry road by the hooves and wheels and could make out a line of trees to my left that marked the course of the Missouri River about a mile away. It was the only green to relieve my eyes anywhere around. And we were gradually moving away from it. The dust did not seem as bad as I had expected. The stiff south wind was whipping it away from the coach to our right. This Dakota soil didn't seem as powdery as some farther west. Then, too, maybe not as many wagons had passed over this road to pulverize the dry soil after the last rain.

Fin pulled out his mouth organ and was wiping it on his shirt-sleeve. He grinned across at me. "How about a little music to liven up this trip?" Without waiting for a reply, he swung into the lively "Garryowen."

The prince seemed to enjoy it.

"I used to like that song before I began to associate it with Custer," I remarked when Staghorn had finished.

"Okay, try this." And he treated us to "Sweet Betsy from Pike." Then I was transported beyond, the hot wind and dust of the rocking coach by the haunting strains of "Shenandoah" and "Londonderry Air." I closed my eyes and leaned back, oblivious to my surroundings for a few delicious minutes.

"Beautiful," I murmured as he finished.

"I'm not really musically inclined," Fin said, pausing and tapping the harmonica on the heel of his hand. "My father can play the fiddle, but this is the only instrument I know much about. Took to it naturally when my folks bought me one when I was just a kid. Besides, it's small enough to carry around. Sure enjoyed it a lot of hours when I was standing those night watches in the Trades." He glanced out at the shimmering waves of heat rising from the sun-blasted plains. "Wish I was there now."

Karl said something to Nicolae in Rumanian; he nodded and fished a deck of cards from his vest pocket. Karl brought the flat leather valise up to rest on the center seat and form a small table. Alex shifted his stocky frame around to join in the game as Nicolae began shuffling. They ignored me and Fin and the prince as if we were not even there.

We stopped every eighteen or twenty miles, as near as I could estimate, to change horses. The way stations were low-roofed sod structures with brush or pole corrals, and were usually located near a small stream. Only one or two had gone to the expense and trouble of having a well drilled.

"The company put up the money for it," a bewhiskered blond station attendant told me as I gulped thirstily at a gourd dipper about midafternoon. "I sure couldn't afford it. Look at this place." He swept his arm at a field behind the sod building. "Crops burnt up for the third straight year. Tried to help me and my missus stretch out what little pay I get—maybe grow a little grain for the stock, and look what happens. Hell! It's a damn race between the weather and the railroad to see which one can put the company and me out of a job first."

All the while he talked, he was helping the driver get the fresh team in harness.

About seven o'clock that evening we finally stopped

193

for supper. There had been no lunch stop, and I was famished. I estimated we had come about a hundred miles from Yankton over the dry, mostly level country. Surprisingly, the station-keeper's wife set a pretty good table, serving up hominy, fresh bread, and what passed for beef stew. It didn't matter; I would have eaten anything that was the least bit edible. Dust-covered and tired of traveling as I was, I felt refreshed and renewed after I had gotten a meal under my belt. This was not to be an overnight stop. The driver and the team were both changed here, but we were to continue rolling right through the night.

The brassy sun still lacked at least an hour of setting when we came outside at 7:45 and climbed into our seats again. I didn't relish the long night of sitting up, but Fin and I had discussed it with the prince over supper and decided that since we were making such good time, we could lay over and sleep a few hours when we reached Pierre.

The south wind that had blown all day now gradually slackened and died with the coming of the sunset and the long twilight that followed. We were engulfed in the choking clouds of dust that billowed in on us from both sides of the open coach. Steamboat travel with all its hazards was looking better all the time. Finally, two and three of us at a time took turns climbing up and stretching out atop the coach to get some relief. Fin and I made sure one of us was with the prince when it was his turn to go up. This long night would be an excellent time for any one or all four of the prince's men to have another try at assassination. But, hard as I tried to stay alert and watchful, my eyes kept falling shut. Fatigue was like a drug that finally overcame me. Fortunately, sleep also got the better of the prince's men, or else they

194

had some other plan in mind. By the time dawn finally came, nothing unusual had happened. They all looked as hollow-eyed as I felt.

"Are you hungry?" Fin asked me as we stretched our stiff muscles at the first stop after sunup.

"You bet. It's been a good twelve hours since we ate."

He looked around for the others, who were standing about thirty yards away, getting a drink. Then he stepped over to the coach and reached under the seat where he had been sitting and pulled out a cloth sugar sack. "Brought along a few things to nibble on. I'd heard about some of the food at these stage stops. Here." He reached into the sack and handed me a small piece of cheese and some hard bread. "Got this at a general store next to the stage office just before we left. Just an afterthought."

My face must have registered my surprise and thanks. The morning sun sparkled on his blond beard stubble as he grinned at me. "Just kinda keep it out of sight. I don't have enough for everybody. And it'd be mighty rude if I didn't at least offer the prince some."

"Can you believe that less than a month ago we were stuffing ourselves with gourmet cooking on the *Silver Swan*?" I said, trying to work up enough saliva to chew the dry bread.

"Ah, well—'Chicken today, feathers tomorrow,' " was his succinct reply.

I ate quickly, feeling almost guilty to be hiding from the prince as I gulped down my food behind the stage. There was nothing to eat at this stage stop—only water. I had a good drink of that to wash down the dry bread and cheese.

Ion, the tall, meticulous Rumanian, had splashed

some water on his face from the horse trough and retrieved a new razor and soap from his luggage and was attempting to shave by feel. He made a bad job of it, nicking himself several times—once on his protruding Adam's apple. The whole business seemed to put him in a sour mood.

Soon we were rolling again, this time with another new driver, a browned, whip-thin man who looked as if he were made of springs wrapped in rawhide. He had a hooked nose, a huge mustache, and a mouthful of chewing tobacco. I decided it was the latter that contributed to his silence as I took my turn atop the coach when we pulled out. He said nothing, but after a time, I decided it was his concentration on his job, as well as the quid in his cheek, that kept him so silent. I watched his fingers walk expertly up and down the lines as he was in touch with each of the four horses, guiding, coaxing, urging them along.

The wagon-track road we were following began curving northwest toward the Missouri again. Now and then we saw wheat fields of some hardy pioneers who had homesteaded this far west into the Dakota Territory. In spite of what appeared to be a drought, the fields looked green-gold and heavy-ripe for harvest. I wondered if they had been able to build some sort of diversion dams on the tributary creeks as a crude method of irrigation. Or was this wheat hearty enough to require only a little rain? Many of the Scandinavian deck passengers who had come upriver with us, I recalled, had been heading north to hire themselves out as harvest hands.

About midmorning I noticed the driver glancing down at the right front wheel. He slowed the team to a walk and peered intently over the side for a few seconds. Then he eased back on the reins and stopped the team completely. The dust caught up and blew past us, leaving only the hot wind and the high sun burning through the back of my shirt. Sweat trickled down from under my straw hat brim. The driver, who seemed impervious to the heat, had set the brake, looped the lines around its handle, and climbed down. I was too hot and miserable to inquire as to what the problem was. I could feel the coach rock as he pulled and tugged at the wheel.

"What seems to be the problem, driver?" came the clipped accent of Prince Zarahoff. I climbed over, stepped on the wheel rim, dropped to the ground, and walked around the rear of the coach.

"Nary a drop o' grease in that hub," the driver grunted, spurting a stream of tobacco juice between the spokes of the offending wheel. "She's drier'n this here prairie and a-squallin' like a newborn babe. We ain't goin' ta get much further without she cool down some and we figure out a way to get 'er lubricated." As he spoke, he placed a hand on the wheel hub and quickly jerked it away. Then he got down on one knee and made a thorough inspection of the wheel, both inside and out. "Don't seem to be leakin' anywheres," he stated. "She just don't appear to have had no grease for some time. 'Taint the first time that damn Clinton ain't checked her out afore she left Yankton. Prob'ly runnin' on a dry axle all the way."

By this time, all seven of us were standing in the hot sun, waiting silently for the driver to decide our next move.

"We ain't but twenty-five miles or so outa Pierre," he muttered, thinking aloud and rubbing his lean jaw. He squinted up the road as if he could see Pierre from here.

197

A dust devil whirled a wavering spiral a half-mile or so away, then began to dissipate even as I looked. The wind whistled softly around the coach, picking up dust from the restless horses' hooves and carrying it away to the north.

Finally the driver seemed to come out of his reverie.

"One o' you grab that bucket hangin' under the rear boot there and fetch me some water from the river. We need to cool this thing off."

The prince gave an order in Rumanian, and the muscular Alex immediately unhooked the two-gallon, brass-bound oaken bucket and set off at a jog toward the river, about a quarter-mile away to our left. The Missouri was low and the water a long drop from the earthen bluffs we had been traveling over. The relentless river had carved a deep canyon in the Dakota prairie and, from our level, vertical dirt cliffs dropped a hundred feet and more to the water. But there was a break in this line of high bluffs just a short distance ahead where a small creek emptied into the river. The land dipped down gently at first, then in a series of broken brown terraces where former floodwaters had eaten the bank, and finally ended in a level spot shaded and greened by several large cottonwoods and oaks. It was toward this inviting place that Alex trotted, the bucket bouncing awkwardly against his legs.

"Any o' you got anything in your luggage we could use for grease?" the driver was asking, as if he expected a negative answer. "Anything atall—like vaseline, creams, or lotions—anything slick or greasy we could use to get us into Pierre?"

We all looked blankly at each other. Our lost luggage had been replaced by only the barest of necessities.

"Hell, I wish we had some women along," the driver

198

continued. "They always carry stuff like that."

The prince, Fin, and I shook our heads. Ion, Karl, and Nicolae looked from one of us to another, as if trying to figure out what we were talking about.

Suddenly, the frown left Fin's sun-darkened face. "I've got a small block of cheese, but I don't guess that would help."

"Cheese? Cheese, you say?" the driver brightened up. He let go a stream of juice, barely missing my right boot. "Why didn't you say so b'fore? Let's have it, man!"

Staghorn dug under the seat for his sack and handed over the cheese, glancing sideways at the prince. But the prince's face was impassive.

The driver pulled out his Barlow knife, opened it, and cut a thin strip from the block of cheese. "Ah, this'll do the trick. I was just before using some green leaves offen a cottonwood or some grass, or some o' my plug to wrap around that hub to ease 'er. But this'll work a lot better." He turned to us, closing his knife and handing the cheese back to Fin. "A couple o' you help me get those boxes outa the boot and offen the top. We need somethin' sturdy to block this thing up when we take the wheel off."

We all pitched in and had the small trunks and wooden boxes wedged in a pyramid up under the forward end of the coach by the time Alex returned with the water.

"We need to get these horses outa the sun," the leathery driver said, pouring cooling water slowly over the hub. "Any o' you know how to unhitch a team?" The prince and I stepped forward. The driver handed the bucket to Fin. "Then help me. Then lead these animals down to the river for a drink." The prince gave another

199

command, and Karl and Nicolae also came forward. But they were nearly as inept as I was when it came to this kind of work. Finally, with the exasperated comments and instructions of the driver, we got the job done.

"Now, don't let 'em get away from you, whatever you do," he warned as the team was led off, two by two, toward the river by the prince, Ion, Karl, and me. Alex and Nicolae stayed to help raise the coach while Fin and the driver worked on the wheel.

We had a little trouble getting the skittish horses down the broken, crumbling terraces, but they were hot and tired and smelled the water and seemed to do all they could to help us lead them. When we finally got them down on the level under the trees in the green grass, the big horse I was leading jerked the lead from my hand and lunged toward the water. I stumbled back out of the way, watching him and the other three animals plunge their muzzles greedily into the muddy current. For a few seconds, I was totally off guard. In an instant, I was aware of my mistake as I caught the shadow of a movement out of the corner of my eye. But it was too late. Pain exploded in the back of my head and I felt myself failing forward into a black pit.

CHAPTER 19

I FOUGHT TO FREE MYSELF FROM A CHOKING, suffocating feeling. Instinct gave way to sudden panic as consciousness returned and my arms sought to tear away the smothering, blinding thing that held me. Ignoring the flashes of sharp pain in my head, I thrashed and twisted myself over. My face was suddenly clear of the water, and I realized I had fallen into the edge of the river. There was the blue sky above, but the tops of the big cottonwoods tilted crazily at the edges of my vision. The stiff crown of my straw hat and the fact that I had moved slightly at the last instant must have saved my skull from being crushed by the blow. My body seemed to be floating, and time seemed to be moving very slowly. I put my arms down behind me, and my hands sank into the soft mud of the river bottom about a foot below me. I *was* floating, and my booted lower legs still lay on the muddy bank.

I let myself go limp in the gently buoyant water, closing my eyes and trying to think through the intense pain, trying to figure out what had happened to me, how badly I was hurt. I opened my eyes again. There was no double vision, and the trees had stopped moving. One of the horses moved near me as he continued drinking. I was sure I was bleeding into the water. But as the seconds passed and the searing pain in my head subsided to a throbbing, I began to feel I was not badly injured.

As my senses cleared, I realized I must have been attacked by Ion or Karl. How long had I been out? It couldn't have been more than a few seconds, or I would have certainly drowned. I put my hands on the bottom to steady myself and half turned my head so that one ear was out of the water. I could hear nothing but the normal sounds of the horses and a few birds somewhere. Was the prince already dead from a quick, silent knife thrust? The thought that I had been so stupidly careless hurt nearly as much as my head. I dared not move. If they were still close by and knew I was not dead, they would surely finish me off. I drew a deep breath and floated limply on my back, hoping that if my attacker was nearby he could not see that my eyes were open. I slid my right hand slowly up toward my gun belt, but my holster that was under the water was empty. My gun must be lying somewhere under me on the muddy bottom. I slid my hands along the bottom without seeming to move, but to no avail. Without my gun, I was helpless. I knew both of them were armed. Maybe whoever hit me had also taken my gun. Had they killed the prince, and were they now joining Nicolae and Alex in finishing off Fin and the driver?

The throbbing in my head made thinking difficult, even though the water bathing the back and sides of it felt good. I let my arms fall back to steady myself against the bottom of the river. A few more seconds passed. I had to move or do something. I couldn't just lie here indefinitely. If anyone was close by, he must not be watching me very closely or at all, or he would have noticed that I was conscious.

Should I shove myself back out into the river and try to swim to safety, and maybe chance drowning in the treacherous current, fully clothed with boots on, or should I just get up and, unarmed, face whoever was up there? Would I be cut down instantly by a bullet? Probably not. If Ion or Karl had wanted to kill me that way, he would have done it already. A gunshot would have warned Fin and the stage driver who were out of sight above. I would more likely get another club or a knife thrust. And I could avoid either one of those if I were quick enough, since I was sure no one was within several feet of me. The horses had apparently drunk their fill. By rolling one ear out of the water I could hear them ripping up mouthfuls of grass as they grazed peacefully nearby.

I decided to jump up and face it, rather than chance the river. I gathered myself for the attempt. It had to be fast. I took a deep breath and lunged over on my side, pulling my feet under me, and splashed and stumbled up out of the water. My head reeled and pounded and the world spun in bright sunlight. As I fought to keep my balance and focus my eyes, I heard the unmistakable double click of a hammer being brought to full cock. I dove instinctively to the grass.

"Get up, Mr. Tierney," an accented, but unfamiliar, voice said. "I'm not going to shoot you—just yet."

I raised my throbbing head and finally focused on the smiling face of Ion about twenty feet away, looking at me over his Colt. Even at that distance, the black muzzle looked like the barrel of a cannon.

"I was waiting for you to get up," he continued in perfect English, tinged with a slight accent that might have been French. "I didn't think I had hit you hard enough to kill you. But I imagine you have a slight headache."

My heart sank, and I didn't trust myself to reply as I rolled to a sitting position on the grass in the hot sun and reached tentatively for the back of my head. My fingers came away from the wet hair with fresh blood. I had a nasty gash in my scalp and the beginnings of a large knot, but my skull seemed to be intact.

The lanky Rumanian crossed his legs where he sat on the huge driftwood log and rested his gun arm on his knee, steadying the weapon on me.

"When did you learn to speak English?" I finally managed to croak, silently cursing myself for sounding so stupid.

"You poor fool. Do you think we did not know what was taking place the entire time? We all understand English, though I speak it much better than my comrades."

As he spoke, I glanced around, trying to see into the deep shade under the trees. As my eyes adjusted to the glare of the overhead sun, I caught a slight movement on the ground near the giant cottonwood. It was Prince Zarahoff, sitting with his hands and feet tied with leather harness straps and a gag around his mouth. He didn't appear to be injured.

"What do you plan to do?" I asked, wondering where the bearded Karl had gone.

"It is unfortunate for you and your friend that you involved yourselves with Ferdinand." He gestured toward the trussed-up prince without taking his eyes from me. "You should have gotten off the boat in Saint Louis with your other friend. But your persistence in interfering, I'm afraid, has now become fatal. I had hoped we could just dispose of this so-called prince"— he said the word with a sneer—"quickly and cleanly and be on our way home, while your government had the embarrassing task of trying to explain how a visiting dignitary, son of the king of Rumania, met an accidental death in this country."

In spite of my pain and my perilous situation, I was finally getting the answers we had guessed at for weeks. And, come what may, I was determined to get the rest of them if I could, even if only to divert my mind from my impending death. Maybe if I could keep him talking, I could stall him and figure some way out of this mess.

"Why do you want to kill him?"

"Ha, you Westerners are very naive when it comes to matters such as these. Your own president was assassinated only a dozen years ago. Why? Because he had become the enemy of the people. It is the same with our so-called king. He has taken all power and wealth to himself. He cares nothing for the people. There have been crop failures and many other problems, but he has ignored the people in his pursuit of yet more wealth and power and the crushing of all opposition." He jerked his head in the direction of the prince. "There sits his only son, who is becoming just like him. Ferdinand is the king's only weakness. He loves that boy. He is in line to succeed to the throne in a few short years. By then the Zarahoff family power may be so strong no one can break it. We must cut the line of succession now. If we kill Ferdinand, the old man's will to live will be gone. He will be easy to dethrone."

"What then? Another dictator?" I asked, my mind only half on what he was saying. I had heard this same sort of talk among some of the radical Fenians who lived in Chicago.

"No," he almost snarled. "It will be a people's government—maybe a republic. We will decide that when the time comes."

"Who's 'we'?" I stalled, holding both hands to the sides of my head to keep it from splitting. Surely someone would come looking for the horses in a few minutes. I didn't know how long we had been gone. I was sure it probably seemed longer than it was. I was sitting cross-legged in the grass, my wet clothes refusing to dry in the hot sun since I was perspiring heavily.

"The four of us represent an organization, a movement, that is determined to free our homeland of this tyranny. We represent the landowners who have been cheated of their land by this so-called king. We were chosen for this mission from hundreds of candidates." He pulled his lean frame to a straighter position, and his eyes glittered. He took off his hat and, with his free hand, smoothed the black hair that was already plastered down carefully to his head. With his long neck, his black eyes, and the perpetual half-sneer on his face, he reminded me of some sort of preening snake, weaving in front of me while holding the deadly gun barrel steadily on my chest.

"What's in it for you?" I asked quickly when I realized he had stopped speaking. My voice was sarcastic. Even young rebels are not completely altruistic. And this man was not that young.

He smiled wickedly. "Freeing my country from its shackles is my greatest reward," he replied, "but the coffers of the royal treasury will be open to us as soon as we take over. In addition, I am being well compensated for the successful completion of this mission."

It's not successfully completed yet, I thought. Not while there was still breath in my body. I wanted to ask him if I could get into the shade, but didn't want him to know how badly I was hurting. The sun was like a drill, boring into the top of my bare head. I guessed from the shadows it was close to noon. I looked around again. "Where's Karl?" I silently held my breath for his reply. If he had gone back to the stage, the three of them could have already surprised and killed Fin and the driver. If that was the case, it was all over for me and the prince. Fin was unarmed—at least he carried no visible gun or knife. But the sailor was resourceful and was constantly surprising me, as he had with the bag of food.

Ion inclined his head to the left. "He is up there keeping watch on the coach." He smiled smugly. "As soon as they have the wheel fixed, he will go ask them, or motion to them, to come and help us catch the horses. Karl and Alex and Nicolae will quickly take the driver and your friend prisoner while they are unsuspecting."

"Why didn't you just shoot us all in the coach and be done with it, instead of all this folderol?" I grated, my anger and frustration rising. My heart pounded in my head.

Ion was his calm, collected self again. "In order to escape from your country unmolested, we must make your deaths appear accidental. If it hadn't been for you and your friends, we could have disposed of Ferdinand weeks ago on the Mississippi, with no one else being hurt. But, because of your interference, you and Mr. Staghorn and the stage driver must also die."

"No sacrifice is too great in the cause of liberty," I replied dryly. He gave me a strange look as if the sarcasm had been lost on him.

There was a scuffing noise behind him, and Ion half turned his head without taking his eyes from me. "What is it, Karl?"

The bearded young man had scrambled down the crumbling dirt terraces and come up to where Ion sat. He glanced briefly at me. He said something in Rumanian, and Ion answered in the same tongue, gesturing with his free hand. Karl looked at me with expressionless, dark eyes and then turned and began climbing back up the broken hillside toward the level plain above. I noticed that he still wore his new-looking gun belt. I glanced back at Ion to see if my own Colt was stuck in his belt somewhere, but it was nowhere in sight. His own gun was rock-steady on his crossed knee.

"Karl tells me they are nearly finished with the wheel, so he is going up to put our plan into operation. When you are all our prisoners, you will rehitch the team, you will all get back into the coach, and we will whip the horses over that high bluff into the river. If the hundred-foot fall does not kill you, you will very likely drown. In

207

any case, we will be there to make sure there are no survivors. When the authorities investigate, my companions and I, who are able to speak and understand only a little English, will let it be known that something frightened the horses and they bolted off the road toward the bluff; and the driver, in spite of all his heroic efforts, was unable to check them before they plunged over. If your bodies are recovered, there will be no bullet or knife wounds—no injuries that could not have been received in the fall. The four of us will survive because, fortunately, we were riding on top of the coach and were able to jump clear in time, with only a few bruises and a little dirt to show for our escape from this dire calamity." He showed his teeth and chuckled, as if unable to contain his mirth at the cleverness of his plan. It was obvious that the gawky, meticulous, soft-spoken Ion whom Fin had picked as the most inoffensive of the four, was really the brains and the sinister guiding force behind the whole plot. I closed my eyes and groaned. In spite of our suspicions, we had been completely taken in. My reporter's instincts had been dulled into a false sense of security over the past days, when I had actually begun to suspect that the prince was a little paranoid.

I glanced over at Prince Ferdinand who was still sitting quietly, not even struggling against the tight straps and the gag. But his eyes were alive with hatred. There was no sign of fear in him.

Ion's face had become serious now and he stopped speaking. Two or three minutes passed with no sound but the birds calling and the prairie wind sighing softly in the tops of the giant cottonwood. Only now and then did any of this breeze penetrate the green oasis where we sat near the river. Ion seemed to have his ears cocked for some sound from above. Several times he even took his eyes off me and glanced toward the waving clumps of grass at the lip of the dirt bank where Karl had disappeared. The horses were grazing at the edge of the shade. It was a deceptively peaceful scene. A sense of quiet isolation permeated the place. The three of us and these draft animals might have been the last creatures on earth.

More minutes dragged by. Ion's expectant look gradually turned to one of grave concern. He slipped out his watch and glanced at it. Finally he replaced his hat and got up from the log. "Let's go." He jabbed the gun barrel toward the bank. "Walk ahead of me."

I got to my feet and fought a sudden wave of dizziness. I walked slowly up the grassy slope to the dirt terraces and began to climb. I could hear the Rumanian a few steps behind me.

"Stop!" came the command from behind me, and I froze where I was, about ten feet below the level of the prairie. "Move to one side." I did as I was told. He crept up to the lip of the bank about a dozen feet away, still holding his gun on me, took his hat off, and eased his head above the top. He stared for several long seconds before sliding back and replacing his hat. "I want you to climb up ahead of me. If you run or yell or try to make any sign of warning, I will shoot you dead. It would be no trouble to bury your body so it would never be found." There was no doubt that he was not bluffing.

I climbed up over the bank and started walking toward the coach about a quarter-mile away. For a minute I was so engrossed in what I saw that I almost forgot the man behind me with the gun. The big Concord coach was deserted. It stood silent and empty in the road where we had left it. Nobody was in sight in any direction on the treeless plain. The boxes and bags were still piled up and wedged under the front axle, so I didn't know if the wheel had been fixed or not. Everything was silent as the tomb.

Something was very wrong. Possibilities flashed through my mind as I walked slowly onward. Was there some sort of ambush awaiting us? If so, from whom? The Rumanians? Had Fin and the driver won out? Maybe they had all killed each other and were lying dead inside the coach. I had heard no sounds of a struggle. But then, probably only a gunshot or a loud scream would have reached our ears. How had five people vanished? The nearest hiding place was several hundred yards onward where the road dipped down into the dry wash of a creek bed that led into the Missouri.

The wind had subsided somewhat and was now coming more out of the west. The sun blazed down on my back and my throbbing head. My mouth and throat were so dry I couldn't swallow. In spite of the heat, a slight shiver ran up my back under my wet shirt. My reluctant footsteps slowed as the coach drew nearer and nearer, and I could hear the ragged breathing of Ion, who had edged up close behind me. I knew he was as mystified as I was.

When I finally got within thirty feet of the coach, Ion reached out and caught me by the back of one suspender and touched the muzzle of the Colt to my back. "Stop!" he commanded in a low voice. Almost at the same time the twin barrels of a 12-gauge shotgun were thrust out the window of the coach, and the voice of Fin Staghorn followed it.

"I've got your friends on the floor in here, Ion. So just step away from Tierney and drop your gun."

A wave of joy and relief flooded over me at the sound of his voice. But the tall Rumanian quickly crooked an arm around my neck from behind and crouched slightly so that any attempt to pick him off would very likely get me, too. "It's a good thing you spoke up, Staghorn," Ion replied, his voice not betraying the intense disappointment he must have felt. "I was just about to put a few bullet holes through that coach to be sure it was empty."

I saw movement as the driver herded the three Rumanians at gunpoint out the opposite side of the coach.

"I said, drop your gun and step clear," Fin repeated. He had flattened himself against the front seat and was balancing the shotgun on the windowsill. The hammer clicked back on Ion's Colt about a foot from my head and I was bracing myself to lunge back and disrupt his aim if he intended to shoot into the coach. But instead, he half dragged me around the front of the coach, out of range of the shotgun, until we could see his three companions sitting on the ground together next to the right front wheel. When he saw us, the hook-nosed driver jumped back behind the rear boot and trained his pistol on the trio who were sitting cross-legged in the dust. Then the barrels of Fin's shotgun and part of one forearm appeared at the right side window. Alex, Nicolae, and Karl looked from us to the driver and back again. No one spoke for at least a half minute. My neck began to get stiff from being bent back at an awkward angle. But when I shifted slightly to relieve it, I began choking myself on the whiplike arm. Sweat was trickling down my face and stinging my eyes. Ion twisted me so that my body shielded him from any gunfire coming from the driver or Fin. I was almost facing west toward the river. There was a haze in the sky, or was it the sweat in my eyes? I blinked a couple of times and looked closer. It *was* dimmer. And the light seemed to have taken on a strange color. I squeezed my eyes shut again. My head was throbbing worse than ever. God, don't let me pass out now, I thought. I concentrated on gathering all my strength, bracing my legs under me and steadying my breathing.

"Looks like this here's a Mexican standoff," I heard the driver say. I opened my eyes. "If'n we stand here long enough, someone's just liable to come along this road."

Ion said something under his breath in Rumanian.

Even though I no longer felt faint, the sky that I could see with my head twisted back still had a strange color. The sun began to dim as if a storm cloud were coming up. But it was like no storm cloud I had ever seen. It was almost like a high cloud of thin and glittering snowflakes. I could see what looked like the edge of a darker cloud moving up fast from the west, even though the wind had died.

Something bounced off my upturned forehead and I flinched. Then something landed on my shoulder. It was the biggest grasshopper I had ever seen. Suddenly they were hitting the ground all around us. It was hailing grasshoppers!

CHAPTER 20

WITH A CHOKING SHRIEK, THE FASTIDIOUS ION recoiled in horror, flailing wildly at the loathsome brown insects that were striking his face and clothing.

The air around us was filled with the whirring, rasping sounds of the flying creatures as millions of them came pouring down from the sky on their long, thin, transparent wings. They bounced off our heads and arms and thudded into the ground like living hailstones.

212

For a second or two I didn't realize I was free of Ion's grip. Then I made a dash for the cover of the coach, my feet crushing and slipping on the grasshoppers that were already beginning to cover the ground. Just as I reached the coach, a gun roared behind me and a bullet shattered the coach lantern near my head. Ion had discovered I was getting away. An immediate answering shot from the driver missed, but the gun roared a second time and Ion spun and dropped. Just as the driver was firing at Ion, Alex jumped up and grabbed the driver's extended arm in his powerful grip. With one mighty yank he jerked the lighter man out from behind the boot, whirled him around, and slammed him hard against the side of the coach. Through the swirling storm of grasshoppers, I saw him bounce off but didn't wait to see him fall as I leapt for a handhold and scrambled up the front wheel toward the top of the coach.

A shotgun roared just below me and Alex went flying backward and hit the ground like a limp sack of grain. Before Fin could fire the other barrel from inside the coach, the giant Nicolae grabbed the shotgun by the barrel from one side, jerked it loose, then thrust it back inside. Even from the top of the coach I could hear the sickening thunk as the stock struck Fin, and then the coach rocked as his body fell to the floor. I had flattened myself on the roof of the coach, crushing a few hundred of the flying locusts. Nicolae turned the shotgun on the dazed driver, who was just getting to his feet, and before I could react, the 12-gauge roared. The driver's body was thrown back by the impact. Without a second glance, I knew he was dead.

So now it had come down to me against Karl and the giant Nicolae. Everyone else was dead or out of action. I was desperate for some kind of weapon. There was nothing within reach I could use. In the dark, whirring cloud of grasshoppers and the confusion of desperate fighting, Nicolae and Karl had temporarily lost sight of me. Nicolae's shotgun was empty, but Karl could have recovered his own pistol or the driver's. Even if none of the three of us was armed, I stood no chance against the two of them in hand-to-hand combat. These thoughts flashed through my mind as I realized my helpless situation. I was only seconds from my death. Nicolae looked around, wild-eyed, swinging the empty shotgun. His blood was up and he was ready to kill. He ignored the grasshoppers that were entangled in his hair. Apparently Fin and the driver had hidden the guns, but the two men below were determined to finish me off before going after the prince. It would be only a matter of seconds before they spotted me flattened atop the coach.

If they were going to take me out, they were going to know they had been in a fight. The adrenaline was pumping, and my decision was quick. With the courage of desperation, I decided that a surprise attack was my best defense.

I scooped up a double handful of grasshoppers that were swarming over the top and falling off the edges. Nicolae had turned away from the coach. I got up, crouched, and sprang, hitting him with both knees. As we slammed to the earth with all my weight on his back, I could hear the air whoosh out of him. At the same time I reached around and rubbed both handfuls of grasshoppers into his eyes and mouth. He roared like an angry bear and struggled to throw me off his back. Out of the corner of my eye I could see Karl scrambling around on his hands and knees a few feet away, looking for the driver's gun.

Nicolae finally staggered to his feet with me still clinging to his back. He was half-blinded and spitting. As he whirled around, trying to reach behind and dislodge me, his feet slipped on the oily, crushed grasshoppers and he fell sideways. I twisted almost clear, but he landed on my left leg. Through the rasping, whirring wings and brown bodies of the millions of insects that still filled the air around us, I could make out the form of Karl about a dozen feet away raising a revolver to fire. I rolled to one side just as the gun exploded. I don't know where the slug went, but suddenly Nicolae was my worry as he twisted his giant body over mine and pinned me to the ground and began slamming his big fists into me. Struggle as I might, there was no way I could get free. I tried to shield my face from the hammerlike blows, but too many of them were connecting, and I could feel consciousness slipping away. The hailstorm of locusts that darkened the sky above me was beginning to blur into total darkness and I no longer felt the pain in my head. From somewhere I heard Karl yelling in Rumanian. The pounding stopped and I could suddenly breathe easier as Nicolae's bulk rolled off me. Karl was standing near the coach bringing his Colt down for a clear shot at me.

Suddenly the Colt went flying as the coach door flew open and slammed against Karl's gun arm. The gun went off with a roar as it hit the ground. Like a bloody avenging angel, Fin exploded from the coach, punching Karl before he had time to recover his balance. A right to the stomach doubled Karl, and a right uppercut cracked against his nose, knocking him back against the rear wheel, where he slumped down, dazed. Nicolae roared and went for Fin just as I recovered my senses and grabbed for the nearest weapon—the dropped

215

shotgun. Swinging it by the stock with all my fading strength, I aimed a blow at the back of Nicolae's head. The metal barrels connected with bone and both my hands tingled with the shock. The big man collapsed in a heap without a sound.

"Where are their guns?" I yelled at Fin.

He gestured weakly. "Front boot."

I climbed up and recovered two gun belts and returned, handing one to Fin. The grasshoppers were still raining down in unremitting fury. We peered through the rasping, buzzing hailstorm at the bodies strewn around us. The burst of energy began to drain out of me, and I leaned shakily against the wheel. Fin opened the door and motioned me inside. I batted the flying insects away from my face and pulled myself into the coach. Fin followed and shut the door, affording us some protection from the small bodies thudding on the roof. Fin's face was a bloody mess. His nose was apparently broken, and coagulating blood streaked the lower part of his face and the front of his shirt. There were slight pouches under his eyes that were already beginning to discolor. Sweat was dripping off my nose and my head throbbed as we sat looking across at each other and panting so hard we couldn't talk. I reached over and knocked two grasshoppers out of his shaggy hair. He grinned through swollen, split lips, and made a halfhearted attempt at wiping the blood from his chin. What hadn't dried, only smeared.

"You okay?" I managed to gasp.

"Yeah." He pulled the gun belt around his waist and buckled it. I did the same, then slipped the new Colt from its holster and checked its load.

"We need to get these two under wraps and see how bad Ion's shot. The prince is down there by the river, and we've got four horses to catch if these locusts haven't spooked them too far off."

He nodded and we got to it before the reaction set in and we were too weak to do anything. Using our suspenders and their belts we hog-tied the half-conscious Nicolae and Karl, laying them on their bellies with their hands behind them, their feet bent up and connected, neck to wrists to ankles so that any movement or struggle would choke them. Ion was a different story. He was still alive, but unconscious. He had taken a .45 slug high in the chest and a few inches to the right of center. He had lost a lot of blood and his breathing was ragged. We dragged him back under the coach for some protection from the grasshoppers and left him, since there was nothing else we could do. Then we fought our way back down to the grassy oasis by the river and freed Prince Zarahoff.

But it was no longer a grassy oasis. As the prince rubbed his legs and arms and tried to get enough saliva working to talk, we looked in amazement at the devastation the army of locusts was wreaking in the grove. The grass was being eaten clear down to the bare ground, and the millions of tiny mandibles could be heard munching and gnawing as they ate the grass and stripped the leaves from the cottonwoods and oaks around and above us. It was a numbing, stupefying, overpowering experience.

"God!" Fin breathed. "Just like one of the plagues of Egypt." Crows and blackbirds, jays, and all the birds we could see were gorging themselves on the unexpected feast of insects.

"What happened up there?" the prince finally managed to ask. "I heard shots."

We filled him in on the fight. He nodded gravely and said nothing.

217

"We'd better get after these horses," Fin said finally. "It may take us a while. But I don't think there's any way out of here for them except the way you led them down."

"We may have some trouble getting them hitched when we do catch them. Look at this." I held up one of the leather straps that had bound the prince. It was nearly gnawed through in several places by the voracious insects.

CHAPTER 21

"WELL, THAT WAS QUITE A SEND-OFF," FIN REMARKED to me as we entered our hotel room, and he threw himself down on the bed.

"I told you Buffalo Bill Cody was a real showman," I replied. I glanced out the open window that overlooked the dusty main street of Bismarck. The banners were still stretched across from storefront to storefront— WELCOME PRINCE FERDINAND—and another one— WELCOME BUFFALO BILL—and still another— BISMARCK—GATEWAY TO THE WEST. Without the banners and the brass band and the crowds that were just dispersing into the various saloons to wash down the dust and lubricate their vocal cords, Bismarck would look just like any other dusty, barren river town on the plains. It was nine days later and Prince Zarahoff had just ridden out with William F. Cody, scout, frontiersman, and showman, in a large party of retainers, cooks, packers, and even a photographer to begin his buffalo hunt.

"Man, this is really beautiful," Fin said with awe, rubbing his hand again across the bird's-eye maple box he had just placed on the table next to the bed. "I still can't believe he gave me this." He opened the hinged lid to expose a nickel-plated, single-action Colt .45 with a four and a half-inch barrel, and a nickel-plated Bowie knife. They had matching staghorn handles and were beautifully set off by the dark green velvet lining of the box. Engraved on the knife blade in a small, flowing script were the words, *"Presented to Fin Staghorn by Prince Ferdinand Zarahoff with Appreciation July 18, 1877."*

"He told me he had to keep the gunsmith hard at it the better part of two days to get those ready for you," I said. "I can still hear what he said—'A man with such a magnificent name as Staghorn must have a set of weapons that do justice to it.' "

Fin grinned. "He didn't know I was just a Minnesota farm boy, turned sailor."

"I think he's beginning to find out that the men in this country are judged by what they do, rather than what their names are or where they come from."

"I don't know why he gave these to me," Fin continued. "You did just as much or more than I did."

"Don't worry. I've got a pretty hefty poke of gold coins in the hotel safe downstairs that shows what he thinks of me. Besides, two thousand of that is yours."

"Yeah," he said reflectively, propping himself up against the rods of the iron bedstead with a pillow. "I'm sure a lot better off than I was after six years at sea. It's almost worth this." He indicated his still-swollen nose and the two black eyes.

"That's the second battered face you've endured this trip," I said. "You were just healing up from the last one. I don't think you've been overpaid." I straddled a wooden chair and folded my arms across the back of it.

"If I were you, I wouldn't take up fighting as a profession—not if you value your health and your looks."

"That's what the Doc in Pierre said when he straightened my nose." He poured himself a glass of water from the pitcher on the nightstand. "You have looked better yourself," he continued. The lumps on my forehead and jaw had just about subsided, but were still bruised. The gash on the back of my head was healing nicely.

Ion was in the hospital at Pierre, and the doctor indicated he would eventually recover, to be tried by an American court, or deported, along with Karl and Nicolae.

"I think we were mighty lucky, considering everything that's happened," I said. "Which reminds me, in all the confusion, you never did tell me how you managed to disarm those three by the time Ion and I came up to the coach."

"Well, we had just gotten the wheel back on with those strips of cheese inside the hub for grease, when Karl comes up and says something to Nicolae and Alex in Rumanian. They started gesturing for us to follow them and started toward the river. The driver and I weren't about to go until we had some idea of what was going on. Then Karl says something like, 'Horses. Must catch horses. Need help. You come!' Well, that startled the hell out of me because it was the first words of English I had heard any of them say. And that aroused my suspicions. If he could speak English and had never done so before, why was he doing it now? I figured he must badly want us to follow him to the river. Besides, I didn't think it would take all of us to catch those horses; they didn't seem that wild. I also wondered why you'd been gone so long. I whispered to the driver that I thought something was wrong. I was unarmed but he was wearing a belt gun. He said there was a shotgun in the front boot under the driver's seat. I stepped up and reached in for it, saying out loud that I needed to get a coil of rope to help catch up the team. At a signal from me, we both drew down on them, before they knew we were even suspicious."

"Lucky for everyone you did, or we might all be at the bottom of the river right now."

"The driver was in favor of marching them down to the river. But I was afraid of some kind of ambush, knowing how sneaky they were, so I talked him out of it and made the three of them lie down on the floor of the coach. We just sat down to wait.

"It's too bad about the driver. But, thinking back on it, there was nothing we could have done to prevent it. Those grasshoppers saved the day."

"Right. But they ruined a lot of other people. Wonder if they wiped out your folks' farm?"

"I'll be heading back south tomorrow to find out," he replied. "At least now I feel better about going home, since I've got a little money and can help them out if they need it. My father's dream was to be a wheat farmer on a place of his own. I hope those Rocky Mountain locusts didn't get his crop."

"The editor down at the Bismarck *Tribune* said this is the fourth straight year they've come out of nowhere and hit big sections of the Great Plains, from Kansas to the Dakota Territory and Minnesota. A lot of the homesteaders have packed up and gone back east. There's nothing that's been invented that can keep those grasshoppers from stripping a farm clean in a matter of hours."

221

"Speaking of the *Tribune,* that was a mighty good story you wrote for that extra edition they put out yesterday. Except you made me out to be a hero when I really wasn't."

"That was just a news article. I still have to write that longer, inside account of our trip upriver with the prince and everything that happened."

"At least now you've got the happy ending you were hoping for," Fin said, taking the shiny Colt out of its box and turning it over in his hands.

"I've sent off telegrams to several big-city newspapers, including my old paper in Chicago and the Saint Louis *Globe-Democrat.* Hope to have a few competing bids for my story."

There was a rap at the door, and I jumped, reaching instinctively for my empty holster, forgetting that I had lost my gun.

The door banged open and four or five grinning faces filled the doorway.

"Are you two gonna sit up here all day?" a bearded man yelled. "C'mon down. We've got some celebratin' to do."

A chorus of voices shouted agreement.

"Looks like you boys have already been into the sauce," I remarked, noting the flushed face of Barney Blue, the Missouri River ferryboat operator I had met the day before. A couple of deckhands were with him.

"Hell, yes. It ain't every day Bismarck gets to entertain a real, live foreign prince, Buffalo Bill Cody, *and* a couple of gen-u-wine, copper-plated heroes to boot!"

Fin barely had time to shove his gift box under the bed before we were swept up and out by the roistering crowd. The tall, blond figure of Phil Swenson, an

222

employee of the general mercantile, loomed up in the crowd. Frank Roody, the small, nervous typesetter at the newspaper, was here. Our hotel clerk joined the throng as Fin and I were nearly carried out the door and across the street toward the nearest bat-wing doors. The town of Bismarck had declared a general holiday, emptying most of its business emporiums and filling its saloons. Nearly everyone I had met since we hit town was in the group, pounding our backs, pumping our hands, and buying us drinks.

"That was one helluva shootout!" Swenson was shouting above the din as Fin and I stood, pressed against the bar in the Bugle Saloon. "Man, that took some guts!"

"We didn't have any choice," I protested. But they were hearing none of that. My reply was drowned in Swenson's yell for the bartender to refill my half-empty beer mug. I caught Fin's eye, and he looked as uncomfortable as I was beginning to feel. There was no escaping these well-wishers. They were as determined to celebrate as a bunch of Texas cowhands at the end of a long trail drive, and we were caught in the middle of it.

"Better go easy on that red-eye," I said, leaning toward Fin, "or they'll be carrying us out of here." He nodded, then pretended to have his arm jostled, spilling about half his whiskey. Someone immediately refilled the shot glass.

"C'mon, Matt, give us that story of the fight and the grasshoppers again."

"Everybody's already heard it and read it."

"Naw. Fred and Silas just rode in. They wanta hear it from one of you. Listen to this, Fred . . . Hey, Matt . . ."

Fin was hunched over the bar, trying to look inconspicuous. The crush of bodies, the smell of sweat, whiskey, and cigar smoke in the close air was beginning to give me a queasy feeling, but I gulped a swallow of beer, wiped my mouth on the back of my hand, and launched into yet another recitation of the wild climax to our trip.

"Pardon me, gentlemen! Please! Let me through!"

I broke off my story as the man directly in front of me was bumped into me.

"Hey, who do you think you're pushin', mister?" There was more jostling, and a familiar voice said, "I'm from *Harper's Weekly,* and I've come to interview these men for my magazine."

"You can wait your turn. Unless you want to step in here and listen right now. They're in the middle of their story. Go on, Tierney . . ."

"I must catch the next train east in an hour to make my deadline, and I must have their story now!" the voice insisted.

It was then the recognition hit me, and I spewed a mouthful of beer across the bar as I coughed and strangled in midswallow. It was Wiley Jenkins! Somebody was slapping me on the back as I choked.

"Okay, okay." I held up my hands. "That's enough. I need some air. Let me go outside and talk to this reporter, and we'll be right back." I grabbed for Fin's arm, but he was already ahead of me, pushing out through the men who were crammed six-deep around us. They reluctantly parted to let us through, and we followed Wiley back outside into the hot sunshine.

We dodged a heavy freight wagon as we crossed the street and came to rest against the hitching rail in front of the land office.

"From *Harper's Weekly*?" Fin and I both howled with laughter. "What was that all about?"

"Well, it was the only way I could think of to get to you. Besides, isn't it nicer out here? Although I hate to break up this hero worship . . ."

"I don't know where you came from, but I'm glad you showed up when you did," Fin said. "I was about to suffocate in there."

"You two look mighty lively for a couple of corpses," Wiley said, with a grin.

"Corpses?"

"Soon as I read about the explosion at Sioux City, I took a train north," he replied, smiling at the dumbfounded looks on our faces. "I was sure I'd just be attending your funeral or a memorial service. But on the way I got a later paper that had a list of the survivors. And there were your names on the survivor list. Seems most everybody was ashore when she blew. So I just came on up to Saint Paul and got the Northern Pacific to Bismarck to head you off. Took me a while, what with train delays and connections. I knew you'd be coming here, and you'd said something about meeting. Too bad I got here just a little late for all the speechmaking—but just in time for the celebrating," he finished.

"What happened to that girl, Ellen Vivrette?" I asked.

"Uh . . . well, she . . ." His grin faded as he glanced away, squinting in the glare of the bright afternoon.

"She had a time of it with that cholera," he continued, "but she pulled through and is on the mend now. Anyway, she's gone to Louisville to stay with her aunt and uncle to recover her strength."

"You still interested in her?"

"Yes" he replied quickly. Too quickly, I thought. "I guess you don't really know a person until you've seen 'em at their worst. And she came near to dying. She's quite a woman, and I plan to see more of her later. She strikes me as a little headstrong, but I think the right man could knock the edge off that or channel it in the right direction.

"We got to talking one day while I was visiting her in the hospital after she had passed the danger point. We got to comparing notes, and it turns out that her aunt and uncle are good friends with some of the people my family and I knew in Louisville. So we have a little something in common. Being from New Orleans, and hearing all about the war from her folks, she's not too crazy about Yankees, so that sort of helped establish me as a Southerner—or at least a Border-Stater."

"Are you going right back to Louisville?"

"Not just now. Told her I'd come visit her at her parents' place in New Orleans in a few months."

I threw back my head in a great belly laugh. Wiley and Fin looked startled. "Ah, Jenkins, you damn fool, don't you think I can see through you by now? You've got a lot of gifts, but a poker face just isn't one of them. What really happened?"

A sheepish grin spread over Wiley's boyish features, and he looked down at his boots. "She has a boyfriend in New Orleans. They're practically engaged to be married."

A few seconds of embarrassed silence followed this admission, and I almost regretted having exposed his bluff. I quickly changed the subject. "Have you forgotten where we were headed when all this business started?" I reminded him.

"The Arizona Territory." He forced a grin. "Well, I've got to be lucky at something. If not love, then who knows . . . ?"

The dusty, windy street in Bismarck could well have been a dusty, windy street in Cheyenne, where we had stood only two months before. We seemed to have come full circle.

"I'm hungry," Wiley said suddenly. "If you two can tear yourselves away from the cheering crowds for an hour or so, I'll buy us all a good meal." There was that old, cocky, self-assured gleam in his eyes. "And then we'll get our plans together for tomorrow."

We hope that you enjoyed reading this Sagebrush Large Print Western. If you would like to read more Sagebrush titles, ask your librarian or contact the Publishers:

United States and Canada

Thomas T. Beeler, *Publisher*
Post Office Box 659
Hampton Falls, New Hampshire 03844-0659
(800) 818-7574

United Kingdom, Eire, and
the Republic of South Africa

Isis Publishing Ltd
7 Centremead
Osney Mead
Oxford OX2 0ES England
(01865) 250333

Australia and New Zealand

Bolinda Publishing Pty. Ltd.
17 Mohr Street
Tullamarine, 3043, Victoria, Australia
(016103) 9338 0666